The Great American Everything

The Great American Everything

STORIES **Scott Gloden**

HUB CITY PRESS
SPARTANBURG, SC

Cover design: Kelly Thorn
Interior book design: Kate McMullen
Proofreaders: Corinne Segal

Library of Congress Cataloging-in-Publication Data

Names: Gloden, Scott, author.
Title: The great American everything / Scott Gloden.
Description: Spartanburg, SC : Hub City Press, 2023.
Identifiers: LCCN 2022038942
ISBN 9798885740128 (trade paperback)
ISBN 9798885740142 (ebook)
Subjects: LCGFT: Short stories.
Classification: LCC PS3607.L65 G74 2023
DDC 813/.6--dc23/eng/20221028
LC record available at https://lccn.loc.gov/2022038942

NATIONAL ENDOWMENT for the ARTS
arts.gov

amazon literary partnership

SOUTH ARTS

SOUTH CAROLINA arts COMMISSION

Hub City Press gratefully acknowledges support from the National Endowment for the Arts, the Amazon Literary Partnership, South Arts, and the South Carolina Arts Commission.

HUB CITY PRESS
200 Ezell Street
Spartanburg, SC 29306
864.577.9349 | www.hubcity.org

For

640 Audubon St.
5950 Annunciation St.
964 Taft Pl.
200 Stonewall Ave. #6
1179 Sledge Ave.

Contents

The Birds of Basra

L ast night Telly was reading to me about the city of Basra. One of her fancy magazines of foreign affairs or social states with a special focus on Iraq. Telly is always talking about the horrors of the Middle East, saying how our occupation is just like what we did to South America in the fifties and sixties—"same through line"—she says. This to say that most of what she read to me about Basra I'd heard before, but one new detail had apparently sunk in: the modern region is hitting temperatures in the 120s—world-record highs, hot enough to literally cause birds to drop from the sky.

In Ms. Fontaine's apartment, the thermostat's set to 86 degrees in mid-August, and somehow there are days when that's even too cool for her. Of course, it's in the 90s outside, so the air-conditioning only needs to run once a day for all of ten minutes to stabilize things. All of this I am used to, made peace with, combat with iced tea and an ethical makeup line Telly loves called Raw Earth —the concealer a duller color, but it doesn't sweat off my skin.

But now this issue of the birds in Basra and Ms. Fontaine's 80-pound frame, of equal skeletal integrity, and I can't not think about how it happens: if the birds glide down, a kind of orbital loss of flight, or if the gravity of their heat exhaustion staples their wings to their sides and they nosedive into earth like lawn darts.

And, if it's the latter, is this what I can expect from Ms. Fontaine? Will there come a day when her bones collapse in front of me, where the police will want to know why in the hell the house was so fucking hot.

My relationship to Marta Fontaine began on a lark, a kind of missed understanding. Telly had me half-asleep one night while she read a report on accompaniment, this practice of older generations in desperate need of part-time support, who ultimately become the victims of relentless swindling. Whole fortunes of countless elders completely capsized by their hired attendants. Jewelry pawned, antiques hawked, until the companies assigning attendants realized that burglarizing comes with so much hassle.

Conversely, by setting up a pay-by-service system where attendees are billed for each itemized need—being driven to the bank, buying groceries, teeth-brushing—then one could easily create a system that monetizes every courtesy.

Telly pushed me back awake and read verbatim from a woman's case: "In one month, I was charged twelve-hundred dollars to have my Brita refilled."

These little payments trickling into streams of money that paid dividends to the attendants in a legal, endless capacity: It wasn't difficult to imagine, with no siblings and my parents out of state. Either one day I would move home, forge ahead in ways never desired, or I, too, would find this kind of help, a reverse student loan to continue my own party.

About the time Telly made her way through another subgroup who had been signing over powers of attorney, I felt a calling. The next morning, I searched out accompaniment services and Ms. Fontaine manifested in under a week.

Telly was less than thrilled.

Aside from the heat, Ms. Fontaine's not unusual. She has no family remaining with the exception of a stepsister in Destin, who's just as frail and keeps her own accompaniment services—she was the one who recommended her sister to Gulf Coast Sanctuary, the group who paired me. Though I like to believe I opened the classifieds that no longer exist and read an ad: "Old woman seeking young woman," "Call here to test your relationship," or something more exacting.

Most of our time gets passed through the machinations of friends, or one sober friend aiding a perpetually drunk one, who opts for a wheelchair when she can walk, who has dizzy spells any time blood collects too long, or might have an erratic reaction to cheese, fruit, bread. Barring these conditions, the woman wants naught: rarefied complaints to have the television louder or blinds lowered.

Now, in between these requests, it's important I keep her life maintained, on the narrow.

I grocery shop, sweep the floors daily, adjust the trinkets of her dresser, make the bed, brush her hair, wait outside the bathroom door for the sound of things falling, and each of these offerings gets entered in and billed along the way.

I'm not entirely certain how the cost of each is eventually covered, knowing some services get run through Medicare and some through her actual accounts. I know there was a late-in-life boyfriend who signed over his pension on his deathbed, but that's not a subject often broached.

On Wednesday mornings, we have one outing, which consists of opening the double patio doors and pushing Ms. Fontaine into the sun—this in lieu of Vitamin D gel caps, which she has a bad track record of swallowing. You'd think the heat, by her measure, would be a welcome sensation, but her complaints of the sun are unrelenting. She wants dark rooms at full heat, like an oven.

"Do you know how turtles fight?" I ask her. "Turtles in the desert?" She shakes her head.

"Telly and I watched about them last night. They're very territorial, desert turtles. They like their own space, and will fight until one of them is flipped upside down on their shells. This is a real checkmate for turtles, because they can't right themselves. Arms and legs are too short. The first turtle to be flipped dries up in the sun."

Ms. Fontaine says nothing.

"Something, right? I wonder about the second turtle, though. If they walk away or just stand there waiting."

On our first date, Telly took me to an Ethiopian restaurant. Food served with sponge bread, no utensils, everything called stew, but poured onto a plate.

"Did you eat food like this growing up?" she asked.

"Food like this?" I repeated, staring down at the shared plate.

"Did your parents cook anything like this—traditional, I mean?"

"My parents are Nigerian."

"But your last name," she insisted.

"I don't know the whole story," I said. "But they were both born in Nigeria."

"Have you ever looked?"

"Looked where?"

"Online! You can go online and find exactly where you're from. That's how I learned I was Mexican," she said.

"What part of you is Mexican?"

"An eighth."

It's now two years later, and this conversation cycles across my thoughts so regularly its threads have become woven, a layer of bedclothes that seem to remain no matter how many times we try to strip them away.

Telly and I live in a cramped apartment in a part of the city that is notably under our means. This wasn't always the case, but once we were out-earning the rent, the thought of leaving for cleaner parks, more space, felt like trading away a bond. More explicitly, Telly believes the worse the part of town you live in, the better chance you have at being associated with the class you identify with. However, if our neighbors could see the eleven-dollar deodorants, the thousands of dollars of kitchen appliances, I sometimes think the association would snap apart; though, maybe they don't even need to see that. Maybe they already know by the way we smell, the way we have energy for their kids running up and down the hall, because inside our apartment there are none. Inside ours, we can afford anything that makes life easier.

"I walked to Marta's today," I say one night.

"That's far, babe."

"About three miles."

Telly nods along on the couch, clicking around for something to watch.

"I noticed a lot of nice places for rent. Some practically in the same neighborhood as Marta."

Telly rolls her head onto the spine of the couch and places a hand on my leg.

"I love you, but no," she says, without even putting her eyes to mine, as if the ceiling should provide a reflection.

"What's the point of living in two rooms when we don't have to?"

"What's the point of using less water when the faucet works?" she says.

"People don't live in poverty when they have money," I say.

Telly lifts her hand off my leg, and puts her eyes back to the television.

"No one here has any idea what poverty is," she says.

The next day, I arrive at Ms. Fontaine's to a terrible smell, one so strong it seems to be cartoonishly inching its way through the keyhole as I unlock the front door. Inside, Marta's chair is in the middle of the kitchen, empty. Moving toward it, I see it's smeared in brown crust, with faint brown heel prints leading down the hall. When I open the bathroom door, she is sitting in the tub holding a wad of toilet paper, likely the combination lock of arthritis and osteoporosis preventing her from cleaning herself.

Without an exchange, I take the papers from her hand and toss them to the sink, dropping my bag in the corner. I motion to let me lift her nightgown off—one of her favorites—a silk print of dandelions that cascade across a beige fabric sky, until the very bottom, where piles of the dandelion images collect into mounds, so that she appears to be inside a snowstorm of flowers whenever she stands upright. It goes in the sink as well, along with her wicker sandals and underwear, and I turn on the shower head, as I prop her arms around my neck.

We stand at the shower with the curtain open waiting for the water to run clear. Marta is frozen, preserved, in her stance.

In high school, to fulfill a volunteering requirement, I took shifts reading to patients in hospice care. Family members were present most days, pushing the shifts into odd hours, either late at night or midday, so that I took advantage of the work and was easily excused from classes, looked upon graciously for doing so. Yet, the patients I read to were always asleep, and the books I read were always my own. They were happenstance listeners. The one thing I remember clearly from that time was how much I wanted them to stay sleeping, how, sometimes, one of them would wake and I would close my book as if I'd just finished and go for the door without making eye contact, even when they started to speak to me. I didn't want to think of them as alive and failing; I preferred them dead.

I turn off the water and pat her body down with little pressure so that's she still damp, but the water no longer runs across her body. Against all instruction, perhaps even laws I was asked to read, I lift Ms. Fontaine's naked body out of the shower and carry her to bed. I place her on top of her sheets and gather new clothes. I set them beside her, and she wraps her hand over my forearm, her eyes tensed by the experience. I pat her hand back.

Billing instructs that we keep a paper record of events, always to be photocopied and submitted each pay cycle, but we update a database online with each service to help automate the process. Whoever built the database must have once performed the duties, because there's an entry for every action, down to shoehorning. In fact, to help place attendants, given the unsurprising level of turnover in the work, the database complies all of the services performed, which then places a patient in a certain class of senility. Inexperienced attendants go with lower senility, the experienced with greater. Though, because of Telly's reading, I know the truer reason for this is because the more direct services entered, the greater the senility class, and the higher the cost of the premium.

In the kitchen, I've lit two candles, both of which turn out to be unscented, and I scrub the vinyl of the wheelchair back to its original color. I pour club soda over the carpet, and, as it sets, I update the log: dishwasher broken, washed by hand.

From the bathroom, I hear Telly make her way into bed, the sounds of smooth magazine paper being flipped.

"I was reading this earlier," she says, "but stopped. It's about Picasso."

I'm not certain what she's picked up, or how we came to be subscribed, but being the highbrow proletariat we are, I'm confident I'm about to learn new reasons to hate Picasso.

"You know *Guernica*, the painting?"

"Sure," I call back.

"Listen to this. Apparently Picasso was commissioned to create an anti-Franco artwork for the 1937 World's Fair in Paris. That was the reason he painted it."

"Oh," I say. "Is that bad?"

"It shows he wouldn't have responded to the bombings if he wasn't asked."

I lean my head out of the bathroom, a glob of lotion across my palms.

"That's not necessarily true. It just means he hadn't made a painting about *Guernica* yet."

"But don't you see how problematic that is? Most of the world associated him with blocks and women up until that point, but *Guernica* politicized him, made him a new kind of revolutionary. Only, he wasn't. He was asked to be that and just acquired it. I'm sorry, but that's a fucked-up truth."

In the bathroom, I rinse my hands and brush my teeth, swallowing down this thought. But I'm not upset. It doesn't seem all that important how the painting came to be, and what about everything else that was made because someone asked for it to be made? For that matter, what is *Guernica* without the bombing? Or, as Telly has said plenty of times before, what is art without conflict?

I get under our covers, where Telly is still on top reading. Serialized columns of 8-point text that I sometimes think she reads nightly only to impress me. Her eyes reddened and yawning, she can't possibly enjoy or process every word.

"I think we should move," I say.

Telly reads a few more sentences, her finger tracing the fine print, as if she's trying to re-locate her thoughts within the article. She finds a break point, closes the magazine, and turns to face me. She has thin lips with no replicable expression, her eyes a degree of light-fastness that tell me she will never change her mind.

"I don't want to have this discussion every night," she says.

"If we moved, we wouldn't have to have it at all."

"The second we move, someone's going to raise the rent here. Someone new will move in, and the owners will decide every other apartment in this building must be worth more. We're not going to be the ones to start that."

"If we move, it doesn't mean anyone else has to move. But we're making more money now. We can afford somewhere nicer."

"I make more money," she says. "You rob elderly people."

Though accompaniment services should inspire more regular shifts than many jobs, most positions are part-time and call for coordinating time off with other attendants. My weekend is Sundays and Mondays, by shared design of a woman named Angeline. Each Tuesday, I take the trash cans Angeline has brought to the curb to the back of the house. Barring any medical emergencies or out-of-town weddings, this exchange is the only consistent confirmation that the other is alive and well.

On this Tuesday, the cans are not at the curb, and so I go down the driveway, where I discover them still in place beside the twines of jasmine. The cans are rarely ever filled, a bag a week of both trash and recycling the average, but, lifting the lids, they haven't been touched.

I turn to see Marta through the kitchen window, standing in a nightgown, the fridge door open behind her. There are days I forget she doesn't require all-hours care, can't afford all-hours care, and that so much of the day still requires her. It's only that time has moved out from underneath her, placing nighttime habits into the daytime, a prolonged wait for the mail to make its way indoors, all her possessions brought down to lower shelves, all her threats highlighted in large print. Every so often, though, I arrive to her animated, almost exclusively cooking with the oven, which is still manageable: set, sit, wait.

I leave the recycling and wheel her trash to the curb.

Inside, back in her chair, I start to ask on it, but she motions me toward the stove and points at the door where the baking light is on. Under the small orange bulb, a glass casserole dish is browning a production of eggs and bread and sausage. She backs up in her chair and hands me an oven mitt.

At the table, I place the dish over a ceramic hot plate I have only ever seen hanging on the kitchen wall and had often considered ornamental. Two plates and forks and cloth napkins are already set out, and we settle in.

From a vinyl pocket on the outside of her chair where Marta keeps the television remote, portable phone, flashlight, she pulls an opened envelope, and hands it off to me, before taking a spatula to the quiche.

The front of the envelope is pressed with the seal for Gulf Coast Sanctuary: two pelicans wrapped as one by their necks.

> *Dear Ms. Marta Fontaine,*
>
> *This is notice to explain that, effective immediately, all services provided by Gulf Coast Sanctuary have been indefinitely suspended for failure of payment. Please understand this suspension is the automatic penalty for any unfulfilled remittance beyond 60 days, per your agreed upon contract. If no installment of outstanding charges is received in the next 30 days from the post-date of this notice, we will be forced to take legal action.*
>
> *For more information concerning your situation…*

On my plate, Marta has placed a square of egg cake and nudges my fork, its steam lifting off in invisible waves.

"Marta—" I say, but her hand goes up. She picks up my fork and plants it in my food.

After we finish our breakfast, she redirects me to the door. I try to speak more with her, but she maintains her silence, even after I offer to stay for the day, if only to put things in order; she waves me away.

As I leave, I kiss her cheek and pull the door behind me.

At home, I discover both a companion letter and an email from GCS assuring me that all outstanding payments owed will be sent as usual despite the unfortunate situation, an act of good faith, and they are enthusiastic about placing me with another attendee. Should I wish to be considered for a different region, I am invited to call the same 1-888 number indicated on Marta's letter. How convenient it must be to have a phone number that contains all known answers.

There's another story about *Guernica* Telly shared years earlier. Not that context has ever been an issue for her when logging a complaint, but we'd been discussing the construction of the new, singular World Trade Center. That week, it had been crowned with a syringe-like cake topper, a push to make it the tallest building in its skyline, and the topic had led us back through the aerobatics of history: Bush versus Saddam, the American ouster of bin Laden from Sudan, 9/11, Bush versus Saddam.

It was on this train of thought that Telly first spoke of the painting, asking if I knew it.

"Sure," I said. "Picasso."

"Well there's a wall-sized print of it that hangs in the UN. It's been there for years, probably put up as a reminder of why the UN exists. It was a few days after Bush announced the invasion of Iraq, and Colin Powell was out stumping his case and held a conference at the UN. They set up right in front of the print of *Guernica*. Obviously, someone recognized the optics, but instead of moving the podium, they put together a large black veil and dropped it over the painting. Just covered it up."

For whatever reason—though presumably our talk the night before—this image comes to mind as I think of Ms. Fontaine. The money's run out, and so down goes the veil. A veil over all her windows, over all her doors, a veil anywhere a crest of light might break in and show the world what's happening.

In a charge, I call Angeline, thinking she must be the only other person who understands this feeling, but she doesn't answer. I call back over the next few hours, send her several messages, but no reply makes it back.

I type and retype a message to Telly and eventually hit send. It occurs to me that I should have texted her first, that many people keep another person around for this very reason, and all the better if that someone sees injustice in everything, but I didn't. Sitting in Marta's kitchen, egg tar burning the roof of my mouth, sitting idly on the bus, she wasn't who my thoughts turned toward.

She responds immediately, and a moon of relief appears:

Fuck that. Be home soon.

"This is the letter they sent me," I say, holding it outward as Telly makes it through the door.

"I'm surprised they only sent a letter, not a phone call?" she asks.

"The support manager also emailed me yesterday, but I hadn't seen it."

"What did they say?"

"Not to feel guilty, that this happens a lot, and many times a payment plan can be set up, so suspensions are often lifted."

"You mean as long as she can pay something," Telly says.

"Exactly. They'll squeeze out anything she has," I say, and Telly nods, goes to the fridge.

"I was thinking I should report what's going on, somewhere local maybe," I say. "I reached out to Angeline, but she hasn't responded."

"Angeline?"

"The other attendant."

"Right. What were you thinking, then, maybe the two of you could picket out front Marta's?"

"No. I don't know really, just seems like I should do something," I say.

"Maybe you should give Marta her money back."

"What?"

"Or, you wanted to live in her neighborhood. Maybe we should switch places. She could live in ours and probably afford the services. You'll get the house you want, commute would be the same."

"I don't think that's fair," I say. "I care about her. I help her."

"You help for money."

"What's happening isn't my fault."

"You should really think about whether or not that's true," she says, and moves past me for the bedroom.

Telly doesn't talk to me for the rest of the night, and I don't try again. We move through separate rooms until we get in bed without reading anything, without watching anything, facing opposite directions, which feels entirely symbolic, to be on the same side but unable to see the same thing.

The week we moved in together, Telly and I both took off work—a sight-unseen decision in that time. We committed to four straight days of making trips between our shared apartments and our new home in lieu of a renting a truck. We ordered fabric samples for a couch and stapled them to the sides of our Goodwill sofa, we taped paint swatches to different walls, we told each other stories about wanting windchimes on both ends of the house, about satsuma trees overwhelming with bloom in the back.

In two years, though, we've been people of little action, little change. The furniture's been bought and the walls recolored, but the sounds and tastes we once imagined live in premise rather than promise. Telly has made the daily atrocities of the world our own intimate atrocities, so much news pervading that the idea of any local progress to our own lives is billed as too selfish to suggest. It all sits in my head, buoys of newsfeeds and guilt hiding the image of Ms. Fontaine, naked, unable to clean herself; the one atrocity that's made contact and Telly still thinks the best response is to stay where we are.

By morning, I haven't slept, and find a message from Angeline:

Hey sorry I missed your calls. Crazy about Fontaine. I think GCS found me a new person near Houma. Some dude. You?

I've never packed for a trip that was longer than five days, and I arrive to Marta's with a large duffel I could barely carry to the bus stop. In it, most of my clothes, a pouch of whatnots, toiletries—much of my grabbing more impulsive than thoughtful, or restrained to areas of the apartment where I wouldn't wake Telly.

Before leaving, I attempted to write her. I sat at the table with one side of myself eyeing the bedroom and the other trying to crosswalk the past and present. The first draft was naturally spiteful, the second an overcorrected softness. By the fourth and final, the letter had become a Post-it, where I wrote simply that I'd be back tonight, like setting a timer for a decision already made.

I ring the doorbell, but realize I've not seen Marta answer the door in five months, always dispatching me to dismiss the pamphleteers. I pull out the set of spare keys I hadn't returned and let the door go wide.

She is sitting at the kitchen table, her wheelchair empty beside her, the tableau of a miracle, but it's truly more like finding someone with their wig removed. She doesn't startle when she sees me, instead waving me in. I put the keys on the end table near the door, needing both hands to pick up the duffel, holding it just above the floor like the belly of an animal.

I take a seat, a cup of hot water sitting in front of her.

"Are you out of lemon?" I ask.

She opens to reply but, seeming to touch on what's going on, seeing the wells of sleeplessness hugging my eyes, closes shut so that her lips make a pop. She directs her chair nearer, parallel parking it until she can move her body in place without touching a foot to the floor. She points me toward the hall, waiting for me to gather my bag, before wheeling ahead and pushing open the door to the guest room.

The house is hot, suffocatingly so. This room, rarely opened, is swollen with humidity. I can feel the first bead break at the back of my neck and run my shoulder blades. Marta wheels back out and pulls the door partway.

I unbutton my blouse and immediately find a small release in only a tank top. Another minute, and I unbutton my jeans, the denim sticking to the sweat around my ankles coming off. I fold them neatly on the bed and sit.

There's no clarity in heat. It's all fever, deliria.

Something that sticks out from the time Telly and I watched the turtles fighting was how the narrator stressed the many ways turtles are evenly matched. They're not biologically interested in evolution or improvement; by land or sea, it comes to pass that though they may be territorial, they don't go looking to expand the empire. Rarely does survival have anything to do with what each turtle is capable of, but rather what each is susceptible to, the many blind spots both physical and intellectual. It's the heat they're up against; it can cause aggression and then demise.

I look to my phone, thinking of the sound of Telly's voice— so much deeper than mine—but she hasn't called or texted. And I know she won't, and I won't, that we will become two silences evenly matched.

Regathering myself, I pull the duffel onto the bed. Unzipping it, everything I own looks too thick, too dark in color. There's no uniform that came with the position, but a complimentary scrub shirt was sent to me upon completing a background check, an ugly yelling blue with a threaded fleur-de-lis spread across the left breast. However, the material had been comfortable, and so I'd purchased several sets from a uniform store. Those I'd left behind, perhaps purposefully.

I take off my tank top and wipe the sweat off my stomach. Understanding something for the first time, I walk in my underwear across the hall and into Marta's room. From her dresser, I find one of her nightgowns and pull it over. The fabric is even thinner and more delicate than the scrubs. It's shorter on me than on her, its thin hem barely past the knee, but somehow the openings in it pull wind from the house, hidden breezes with every step.

In the living room, Marta only smiles when she sees me.

The house is in fair order, but I continue to tidy all the same. I recover my keys to a set of hooks by the door, fix the afghan on the couch, and pull the vacuum from the closet, running it just long

SCOTT GLODEN | 17

enough to put new streaks into the carpet. I place her many water glasses in the sink, scan the fridge, add to the grocery list by the phone.

There are two saved voicemails listed onscreen, so I press play. The first is an autodial; the second is her stepsister, insisting she call her back, saying she can help pay for the services, at least for a little while.

I clear the machine, and watch as Marta angles her wheelchair around the kitchen counter struggling to move past the dining chairs.

"Here," I say, pushing the kitchen table closer to the wall to make room for her, for me, to pass. I walk us onto the patio and edge her out from underneath the awning, so that just her feet touch sun.

"Do you need sunscreen?" I ask.

Marta flicks her hand in the direction of the house. Usually, she keeps it holstered in her chair, along with the remote and portable phone, diligently putting a dab on each age spot like they may still undo. Though the pockets of her chair are flat.

Inside, I find the remote and phone on the coffee table but no sunscreen. I don't find it in the medicine cabinet or at her bedside or dresser either. It's not in the kitchen or set out anywhere visible. Checking the guest room, I quickly finish unpacking, spreading everything out so that each drawer has something. The closet has no hangers and so I leave the empty bag as its only content, placing my sweated clothes inside it like a laundry hamper.

Seeing it all strewn to the open, it occurs to me Marta may not have been gesturing to the house. She may have been explaining there was no more sunscreen, that it only took a single night for something once relied on to run out. I'm still too sweaty to redress, so grab only a bra and begin to debate what it will be like to walk to the store wearing only this sheer curtain.

But back on the patio, she's wheeled herself farther from the house. She tilts her head back, the sun piercing down to dry her up for good.

What is Louder

My brother tells me the bombs don't look like they did on television when we were young: They're not bowling balls with wick spouts that fire out like a sparkler. Instead, they're clock radios; they're wads of Silly Putty with electromagnetic current running through sparse wires; they're ramshackle, he even said—so much so, a bomb looks more like something you store in the garage, which you don't need every day but keep around in case of emergencies.

In the mail office, diagrams drape several walls between the customer lobby and the distribution lap in the back. They depict a suspect package: a bark-and-twine-colored cartoon with long dimensions in a matrix of white. Beneath it, the poster suggests several numbers one might contact, but personnel have a different directive. Call the bomb squad.

These officers, when beckoned—for any number of reasons from chemical threat to live animal—enter the back office, place the package into a vault, and load it into an armored vehicle, their outfits weighted in heavy, proofed material.

The first time they came, Yun looked over to me with outrage and said, "Well, Jesus-motherfuck-me. It's a good thing these guys have all day to dress up like goddamn Robocops, while we wait here in mesh."

"Do you want to be the one opening the package?" I asked.

"The fuck you know I don't, Tom. But I'd feel a lot better with a football helmet on is all."

There's a picture on my desk of my brother and me at Lake Walton, in Provo, Utah. A place we stopped at once on a cross-country drive ahead of his deployment from Fort Lewis, propping our camera on the hood of the car, setting the timer mechanism, and running to a scenic point for a short embrace. I framed mine and gave my brother another print when he first left for Pakistan.

"You can put it in your helmet," I told him.

"Are you trying to remind me of what I look like with hair?" he asked, and then he kissed the plank of my head and went back out onto the deck, where Spencer and Russ were loudly comparing Elizabeth Shue movies around the firepit.

"*Cocktail*. If it's not *Cocktail*, for the name alone, I don't want to play this," Russ continued.

"Danner," Spence started at my brother, "putting aside *Leaving Las Vegas*, which we all agree upon as one, what's the number two movie where Elizabeth Shue is the hottest?"

Through the frame of the conjoined kitchen windows, the blinds of which shredded the image of the men, my brother leaned back in his seat, his foot on the edge of the bowl of fire. He picked up the half-filled bottle, its neck lithe in his fingers.

"Easy. *Back to the Future Part II*," he said.

The two men looked at each other discomfited.

"Danner, I swear to shit, if you weren't able to disarm a bomb the way you do, I would not trust you to water my lawn."

In elementary school, my brother developed an exceptional fear of any vehicle capable of moving. This impairment erupted from nothing, soundless and aggressive: one morning, he wouldn't get in the car; the next, a plane flew overhead, and Robbie entangled himself in cones of sumac trying to hide out from it. My mother, who was a woman of little patience to begin with, lost it. She denied him dinner and breakfast for three full days, thinking this would straighten him out, and Rob had to survive on the bologna sandwich my mother packed me alone for lunch. On the fourth day, she caved. She cried, said everything short of an apology, baked my brother a cake, weighed down in buttermilk, and found a therapist within walking distance of our house.

For three and a half months, my mother and father took turns walking Robbie between school and the psychologist, guiding him away from traffic, so that he could sit in a small, poorly lit room with Styrofoam ceiling tiles, discussing his alienating condition with a man defined by his mustache.

As the older brother—notably by one year and several hours, born to the same day in March—I tried to take charge the best I was able and rein in the heckling my brother's fears provoked.

For example, my first and only fight came and went in the sixth grade, when I punched Marc Suspin in the bottom lip, an as-seen-on-TV-haymaker, dislocating his jaw so that he had to drink a month's worth of meals through a straw.

One day after school Marc had chased my brother down on his bike, tormenting him along the way, until popping a wheelie onto Robbie's calves so that his body slingshot into the concrete walk. Rob's face bled in every quadrant, his cheek on one side scraped open like a zipper. I wasn't far behind when I saw it happen, and chased Marc down before he could get his bike steadied, pushing through him with every knuckle, knocking us both headlong into the Berrys' yard, their tufts of grass immediately reddened with the result.

Of course, as time lagged and seasons mutated, so did Rob's fears. They lessened, they freed. Once my brother was able to overcome his milder hesitations, we discovered he held no hesitations whatsoever when it came to the outer bounds of danger. He fell from every height, dove imperiously into local lakes; Rob so outgrew the world that he shrank mine. We lived together in the same expanses, only he made it seem like my perspective was glued up inside a snowglobe.

Just over two years ago, I was promoted to the position of agent at our municipal post office. It became my responsibility to locate and retrieve all missing packages, which were either en route to us or had left our dispensary and disappeared. I was the youngest person ever to achieve this role of odd esteem, and my assigned deputy agent was Yun, a Korean émigré, who continues to core out the soft spots of my head and hammer against them from midday on.

The job, admittedly, isn't as noteworthy as its title. People call, we answer. Occasionally, we'll get a letter about an undelivered package or a package that's been rucked apart in transit, but, in unquestion-able irony, these letters often show up to our offices too late.

As soon as the doors unlock at eight, the phone begins to ring. People believe, since we are just opening, that it's the best time to call: first in line, they think; early bird, they think; but since they all think it, this is our busiest time. By ten, we usually have our case-load for the day, and the phone goes still.

Yun, though you wouldn't think it, is our customer service honcho. He pretty much lives on the phone, and he does it with unthinkable tact. As soon as he hangs up, he sounds like the least decent man on earth. Yet on the phone, his elocution, his naturally conciliatory voice, it all comes out in shine: "Mrs. Rosenblatt—I'm so glad you called, and we're going to get to your missing package in a moment, but first I need you to tell me when I'm going to see your little Cotter again."

Another facet of the job involves the examination of parcels. When someone sends out a flat, there's little we can do to disrupt its movement: razorblades, cocaine, acid tablets, ransom letter—a person can mail whatever the hell they please, if it's of a malleable grade. Packages, though, go through a less trusting process. We have scanners, we have biweekly dog sniffers, we have infrared, and we have human intuition. And while this last tool may not seem as useful by comparison, it led to my promotion.

It was two years ago, just before close, when a woman with straight blond hair, a black business suit, and obsidian sunglasses came in with a small, square box the size of an ornament. It was addressed to a man, with a return label for a local P.O. Box. She paid, smiled, and I watched as the red undersides of her beige pumps disappeared through the series of glass doors. Yun had been sorting stamp books alongside me, his counter closed.

"You think Susan would want a pair of those shoes?" he asked me.

"What kind of shoes?"

"Typical man. Those shoes: red heel, shiny skin-color everywhere else."

I had become distracted with the package—the P.O. Box was number 620. Our own units only made it up to 300.

"Maybe it's a P.O. Box at a different office," Yun suggested.

"She went to a post office where her post box isn't?"

"Shit, I don't know. Sometimes I go to the grocery store that's farther out."

"That's only because Susan works there."

"All right, yes, but she's never going to go out with me if she doesn't see me on the regular. Maybe this woman is flirting with you. Maybe this is the beginning of all sorts of packages from P.O. Box 620 and the woman in the TV shoes."

I had already walked away from Yun's prattle and carried the package to the distribution center, which was all but a ghost town at that hour. Out of sight, I shook it by my ear: A dull, thuddish sound kicked back. Despite my better judgment, I called the emergency number, which brought my boss away from her kids on her day off, away from cooking dinner; it alerted the local officials of the township down to the comptroller; and it sent in a three-man SWAT team, swathed in black astronaut suits.

In the commotion, Yun appeared, just in time to see the men ambling slowly toward the package, like dogs closing in on a fox.

"Who the fuck are these guys?" he said, which our boss, Leslie, declined to answer, the spit up of roast beef still wet on her blouse.

In the box was a grenade. A string, which pulled the pin, was attached to one of the cardboard flaps, so that whoever opened it would have just enough time to realize what the flannelled bulb was and think about either the person they loved most or the person that hated them most. Perhaps the only circumstances under which it would be convenient for this to be the same person.

Leslie put her hand on my shoulder.

"We may work in a post office," she said, "but you are about to become a legend."

The first time a device exploded, my brother saw Spencer's knee-cap shoot up into the air like a geyser and fall into the white dust. He said it was clean and dry by the time he reached it: a piece of Pompeii, he called it. Spence lost both legs and woke twice, muttering loose the pieces of a memory no one could recognize, before going under for good. Rob told Spence's wife, Adelaide, that his last words were, "I love you, honey," and he didn't turn back.

It was a common thread in their military storyline, a recounting of last words—only ahead of time. All the men had seen enough, had heard enough, and had had enough to decide their preemptive sentiment. There was no need to die thinking about what you were going to say.

"So, what would you say?" I asked him.

"That it was good. That everything, everyone, it was all good."

My brother's statements since leaving for Pakistan—since his child-hood fears crawled away, in fact—had become mournfully flat. Words held their concise truths: love, matter, right, trust. He had decided upon an experience with each and was tangled in these abstractions. For a time, it upset me. I suspected the tours in Afghanistan, and now Pakistan, where he taught bomb disposal to locals, were not the ideological sound he had responded to, but just another facet of wartime, which rolled over him with its consequence.

Eventually, though, I gave up caring about anything other than Rob's homecoming. I became him, I suppose, normalized to the attrition of language: home, safe, whole, love. What was gaudiest would have to survive.

For a little more than six months, Yun had driven ten miles out of his way to shop at the Kroger's where Susan worked. He would check for her aisle on the way in and choose it on the way out; he'd give her the warmest customer-service, deputy-agent-of-missing-packages voice he could. In the days he planned to shop, we would rehearse his lines, me as Susan, Yun as Yun.

"I've been thinking about upping my approach. Listen to this: Susan—what do you say we toss these groceries in the back of my Mercedes, and we have ourselves a picnic."

"Mercedes?" I ask.

"I just think if I say Nissan, it won't sound as cool."

"What if it actually works, and she goes out in the parking lot with you."

"Then I say my car was stolen, and I'll look to her for emotional support."

Despite our closing earlier on Saturdays, Yun and I are often stuck working as late as six, since the phone rings nonstop, with most people on their day off.

After business hours, Yun will man the paper board, reviewing the timetables of the drivers, making sure anyone who needs a shift off, or replaced, has it, while I run what Leslie calls "the glory eye" over the boxes awaiting transport. It is, potentially, my least favorite part of the week because it entails a rather acrobatic charade on my end—a balance of boredom and attentiveness I can never quite achieve.

Though there are occasions on which a name or place in an address culls out from me a moment in time, and I can lodge myself in a past tense I might not have otherwise found. Lake Walton, for example, was one of those tiny grooves of map I had never intended to see, but came upon while driving Rob from our father's funeral in Arizona to his base in Fort Lewis.

It had been a quiet affair, lacking the usual ceremony of a funeral. In my father's will, he had stipulated that he would like to be buried whole, he would like no showing, no wake, and to be interred in a casket that would not outlast the dirt it was put in. The last of these requests came as no surprise, as our father was always a generously practical man. If he ever found gold, he'd likely be quick to give it away; otherwise, its weight would only serve to hassle him.

At his age, my father, in his balsam box, weighed no more than a hundred pounds, and Rob and I carried him handily between the hearse and resting place, a hastily arranged plat of red, salt-slick earth. We questioned if it even contained strata, or if he was being lowered into a dry riverbed, which would one day fill and float him back to the surface—precisely what he never wanted.

Our mother had died a decade earlier, and her funeral was in part, we suspected, the reason for my father's final demands. Hers had labored on for a year of visitors and dedications—down to a traditional unveiling, which our aunt, my mother's sister, had staunchly insisted on seeing through, despite my mother's listlessness toward religion. It was as if my father could not outwalk the grief and had become trapped in its afterimage.

Oddly enough, Rob and I felt stable after our father's passing. It was an inevitable tone that rang strongly in our ears and then dissipated, and we knew we wouldn't have to hear it again. Not to say we didn't love him to the point of fandom, but we had formed our own unit as brothers, and watching our parents retire to Arizona was, in some ways, the end of what they had been to us.

Driving north, I would have never jerked the wheel out of Rob's hands, taking us abruptly down the center of the off-ramp, if it hadn't been for the Saturdays when I glimmered the names of all the places where mail had come and gone, if it hadn't been for a long, thin box labeled only with the return address of a body of water, as if to say: Should this package never arrive, then return it to the sea.

It was Tuesday when I had last heard my brother's voice. He had called from some international outpost where the background noise seemed part movie, part bug zapper, where telex lines were the mode of communication for everyone but Rob.

"It sounds loud there," I told him.

"Yeah. Pretty loud. Listen, you get a package from me at all?"

"A package?"

"Tommy? I can't hear you. I asked if there was a package from me over there."

"Yun," I said, calling up to the front. "Did you see a package for me today, something from Rob?"

"Sorry, boss. Nothing like that."

"Rob, there's nothing here," I said, uncapping my hand from the receiver and speaking into it sideways, as if to mimic how I thought he was probably doing it.

"Good, good," he said. "And you let me know if something shows up?"

"Well, I don't know, what's the number to Pakistan?"

"That's a good point."

Rob handed off the phone to another officer, who yelled each number codified to a word. My ears went numb listening to him, and I looked down at some seventeen digits that I'd written blindly out of line, so that they made a kind of graphite constellation on the desk calendar.

A week later Yun called me from home, his voice ecstatic and overblown. He was a half-hour late.

"You are not going to fucking believe who is asleep in my bed right now."

"Bullshit. I don't care if you're late, just don't drag that poor woman into your lies."

"I'm not lying! I gave her the line from the other day, and she laughed that I was willing to say Nissan!"

"Yun."

"I'll prove it. I'll take her picture."

"I have no idea what Susan looks like. You could have any girl in your bed and could call her Susan."

"Fuck, you're right. I know! I'll take a picture of her license."

I told Yun that he could have the day scot-free, provided he showed up with a picture of her license. I figured, even if it was a lie, he was the kind of person who would spend the day tracking down a Susan somewhere and convincing her to give him a snapshot, just to prolong a sense of magic.

The line of customers came and went, and I put the open cases we had left into a pile on Leslie's desk for review, which was really in case Leslie stopped in having forgotten something. This way I would look busy, and she could feel the pressure of being behind.

Whenever you work the front counter, the hours hang themselves. What was nearly an entire day seemed like less than a morning, and I almost felt thankful for the break from Yun and everyone else.

The accumulation of packages for the day rested in a canvas

laundry cart. It was past the final pick up, which meant the drivers wouldn't do more than trade their trucks out for their cars, but I decided to sort the dozen-plus boxes onto the shelves and tag the drivers' names to their outgoing parcels for the next morning. It saves them time and, when I'm feeling productive, I like to make this gesture.

I'm unusually fast at my job when I'm alone, as if the deafness of the place mobilizes me, and I'm wondering about the role of silence when I find the package—MAIL TO: TOM DANNER, GOODLETT, TENNESSEE / MAIL FROM: ROB DANNER, PESHAWAR, PAKISTAN. All the lettering ornate, the kind Rob was always practicing before his initial deployment. I would come upon him in the kitchen, where he studied languages like Farsi and Urdu, whose fantastical lettering were all more impressive than our own.

"They use the wrist," he said. "Not the fingers."

The package must have been on the shelves when Rob thought it arrived, and neither Yun, nor I, had paid enough attention. I carry it over to my desk, its shape lightweight to my palm. Once, Robbie had filled a box of sand and shipped it to me: no explanation, nothing hidden inside; it was just a box of the desert he thought might seem funny.

I find the number and dial out of range, where an operator has to connect us manually—I imagine makeshift power lines beneath a sagging camp, long wires stabbing into stereo ports. Her voice is blank and distant in tone, but with a tenor and pronunciation so clear, she could be in the back of the warehouse, whispering. Finally, the lines connect, but the sound on the other end is a hurricane, it yells out of the receiver with inanity and concussion, until I have to hang up.

I redial, the operator whispers to me once more, and the sounds of a pageant war swallow my ear before cutting short on their own.

Considering the infrequency with which I speak to my brother,

I give up. With a box cutter, I slice the tape at either edge, and pause. Slowly a conversation comes back to me, distorted, when my brother explained his outfit would send mail only from registered bases. Several men, in the months preceding my brother's departure to Pakistan, had been captured and held for ransom, their ears and fingers severed and shipped to their families as proof, and the families were sending boxes of money back to the return addresses—keeping quiet as they were told. None of the men were found alive, and the new protocol was instated.

On the wall in front of me is the poster for suspicious packages, its caricature of mail an oddly unblemished version of the box under my hand, on which the letters of my name are centered.

I breathe deep, a reluctant pause where I already know the future but want to put it off anyway, and I call the emergency number. Within minutes, the warehouse is quietly cordoned off and scanned from end to end, the box in a lead vault that rests on a hand truck. I'm answering questions about the date of delivery and the ways the package could have entered the area, and I'm repeating everything twice to Leslie, whom I have on hold and keep returning to, when the phone at my desk rings.

Unnecessarily, I run to it.

"Rob?"

"Tommy. You called here? What's wrong? You okay?"

"The package came, Rob."

"A package came for me, from Pakistan?"

"No, no. It's addressed to me."

"Addressed to you?" His voice is shouting over the line.

"Yeah. The return address is your name."

"Tommy. You listen to me. You get the fuck away from that box, you hear me? Just get rid of it, you hear?"

Behind me the task force is strapping the vault and preparing to load it onto the armored truck. I can faintly hear Leslie's voice calling out my name from the phone near the loading dock, but I'm waving my arms at the men surrounding the vault.

"It's a bomb!" I tell them, "Get away from it!"

Only this is exactly what they're expecting, and so they simply begin to move more certainly, working where they stand rather than transporting the vault and running down time.

Within seconds, they have the box split apart, its sides collapsed and widened out, crumpled newsprint at their feet. Only, there's no bomb. On top, in a plastic bag, is the picture of me and Rob at Lake Walton, both in a look of daydream, its edges crinkled from the way it's been pinned up inside his helmet, a firework of creases pathless over the matte, a tiny catch sight where the sun explodes behind us and the water can't even handle its reflection, so that the lake looks a ruffled yellow. In red pen, an 'X' is drawn over Rob's face.

I run back over to the phone to tell Rob it's all okay, that it's not a bomb or a limb, but the line's cut off, and I can't get it back.

The Great American Everything

New Mexico is the fifth largest state in America. Average highs of ninety, average lows of twenty; the difference between night and day can carry forty degrees in some corners. It has the least amount of water area in the country, clocking in at a lean 230 square miles of landlocked pools. It's goddamn moony. My grandfather once told me, unprompted, that New Mexico has more cactuses than it has humans. He found a sense of longing in this fact, though he'd never been.

"Isn't that common?" I asked.

"Common?" he said.

"Aren't there more trees in Wisconsin than there are people?"

"It's a cactus. A cactus isn't a tree," he said.

I long remembered him saying this, but never saw its overlap in my life, too young to understand the mechanics of a future. Instead, I just kept growing up, just kept heading through the motions without his comment in mind: a solar eclipse in second grade; a participant ribbon at a fourth grade science fair; a last-place finish at the eighth grade spelling bee on the word asparagus: a-s-p-e-a-r...; first kiss in tenth grade in a closet with someone on swim team; college; dishwashing; more college; a graduate degree in biology, and before I was handed that diploma I stood in the emergency room holding my grandfather's hand, watching the life pump in and out of him. I watched all the resilience a man could survive a life with stockpiled and erupt in one last scene, in a presentation to his grandson that said you fight you fight you fight.

When I arrive in New Mexico, however, he's been dead six days, and there's not a standing cactus for a hundred miles in any direction. I ask someone at the first restaurant where I stop, which is partly attached to the train station.

"Cactus? Sure," a waitress says, and walks away into the kitchen. A moment later, she reemerges with her apron loosed and cuffed around her wrist, and leads me through the exit by the bathrooms.

"See?" she says. "Can't miss them."

Out ahead of me, dots of sage and brittlebush tier in the distance. Squinting through the sun, hundreds of cacti slowly become apparent, though none are higher than a boot—all are swollen mounds of needles buried in the rocks.

"Oh," I say. "I was thinking of taller cacti, columnar."

"Saguaro," she says.

"Yes, exactly."

From behind me, she reaches over and places her hands on my shoulders, guiding my frame until my feet point westerly.

"You're one state short," she says, and goes back inside.

⊙

Truthfully, I don't know why I'm in New Mexico. Not an escape, not a terminus; it all rests on a comment made by a grieving woman. At my grandfather's repast, I was sitting beside my grandmother on her blue leather couch attempting to spoon-feed her cold cuts. After failing to do so, I looked for small talk, and thought to share this memory of the cactus, the same one I've always kept neatly folded in that mush of memory you don't ever touch. I said:

"Do you remember him saying that?" to which my grandmother only shrugged, before saying:

"Well, he would know. He lived there."

"He lived in New Mexico?" I asked, and silence—a concrete-poured-down-her-throat silence. For the next twenty minutes, we sat there until she slowly began to pick at the bologna.

On the drive home, I asked my mother and brother if they knew what she was talking about, about his living out west. Both just laughed.

"He flew to Niagara Falls for your aunt's wedding, and never left the state again," my mother said. "Wait," she said. "That's not true. Manny, what did he tell you the other week?"

"He told me he once crossed into Michigan's waters. He said that counted," Manny said.

End of the line.

Only, a day later, the night before I'm set to fly back to Tennessee, Manny, as little brothers will, entered my room without asking, and, as little brothers do, shook me awake.

"Look," he said. An inch off my nose, Manny stretched tight a piece of computer paper. From my bedside I fumbled on glasses, and slowly the snaking blurs of text grew into discreet, pinpoint sans serif:

Miranda, Felix Age: 24
Registered: Democrat, 1956
County: Santa Fe

"Can you believe this?" he said.

"You don't actually think this is him?" I laughed, turning the paper over to see if any other information was listed—address, phone, height, anything—but it was only this line of everyday evidence.

"Of course I fucking do. I paid $59 to expedite some online public records service."

"Manny, he married grandma when he was 18. They had two kids by this age."

"So? Maybe he skipped out on them—just for a time. Maybe that's why she didn't talk about it."

"Okay. Let's say that's true. He abandons his family, moves across country, registers to vote in a primary, and, what? Drives back?"

"Why not?"

"I've lived in Tennessee for seven years and still have a Wisconsin license. People don't register to vote with a motel address."

Manny squats down from his excitement.

"Fuck. An hour ago sixty dollars felt like nothing to solve a mystery."

And, again, that should have been a natural end. Your little brother mistakenly ventures beyond a paywall on a bad lure. Yet, the next morning, I woke to three new sheets of paper spread across my bed: a donation to the Salvation Army by Felix Miranda of Santa Fe; a New Mexico landline number for F. Miranda dated active in 1956; and a newspaper article whose fuzzily loaded caption identified a "Felix Miranda" supposedly third in line from left to right. That last clipping is an image traumatized by sun exposure and scanner streaks. It's as reasonably a picture of our grandmother as it is our grandfather, but something recognizable is contained, some private feature of lineage I can admit to if I allow myself. On this last piece of paper, Manny had written:

"Maybe this mystery is just going to cost a lot more."

Inside the restaurant, I order a plate of tacos and settle into a booth. From the depot, I'd recovered a handful of pamphlets from one of those magazine racks that only ever exist at a depot. The Museum of Indian Arts and Culture, the International Museum of Folk Art, the Georgia O'Keeffe Museum, the Museum of Contemporary Native Arts; each laminate page inviting an appropriate distraction, a stay of execution for an impulsive airline change fee with no legitimate second foot.

"Was it just the cactus that brought you?" the waitress asks, refilling my water.

"Kind of," I say.

"Who told you they were out here?" she asks.

"My grandfather."

"Grandparents mix up that sort of thing. I had a grandmother who believed in ghosts."

"Sure," I say.

"Here long?"

"Just the night, I think."

"And you came in winter. No one comes in winter."

Assessing the stack, she lands a finger on the Georgia O'Keeffe Museum, sliding it out from the others like a magic trick.

"That's the one to see," she says, and moves on to other customers.

⊙

In late November, Santa Fe is an ice rink. No snow, no textured cold, but the air is sharp, and the angles of the desert unknowable, frictionless. From every vantage, it looks like a dimension that leads lengthwise into the past.

The city's main square is a tourist bunker, one catchall peddler after the next, with turquoise and leather in overwhelming demand. Thinking I should have something to show from my trip, I concede to purchasing a small throw rug, something just larger than a door-mat. It has that overstated geometry and diluted, sunset color you can't help but associate with the Southwest.

"Is it a gift?" the cashier says.

"Maybe," I say, reasoning it's a gift to myself, and without asking, he carefully rolls the rug, and wraps it in dark, vellum paper, tying on two lashes with shoelace knots at either end. With the packaging, the rug is too fragile to fold in half, and too wide to keep tucked under my armpit, and so I walk the square with it leaned against my shoulder like a resting bayonet.

Manny is six years younger than me, which has set us on different paths. We've always existed one school apart, no overlap in interests, friends, even love. Yet, I possess more memory around Manny's life than my own. In fact, he is the first memory I can link up with-out dispute, as I waited for him outside the delivery room with my grandparents. That's where it all begins, inside a small hospital room, where a nine-hour labor became a 45-day entreaty to the gods in which we do not believe to spare my brother's life.

"Hyper-vent-ill-ate," my grandmother said. "It's like when you stop running and can't catch your breath. Only he's not running, he's trying to sleep."

What caused this ailment was, evidently, luck. You either have it or you don't, and Manny's chromosomes just turned out to be a big red X.

When it was determined he would survive, be able to manage this syndrome we couldn't pronounce, we all went home and made a plan. My parents instructed me to all the warning signs, which carefully added up to Manny going breathless, Manny going blue, Manny going blue and breathless.

"What do you do?" my mother asked.

"I yell."

"What next?" my father said.

"I push his chest."

"What first?" he corrected.

"I prop his neck, then push his chest."

"Good," my mother said.

Only, in the next three years everyone somehow turned on each other. Manny required a CPAP machine, which whistled all night, the feedback sailing through the speakers of the baby monitor so that we never slept. During the day, there was no childcare service we could afford, and so my father began traveling for better paying work, taking on months-long shifts in remote Pacific ports. Each time he came back more harried, more exhausted, until he didn't come back, and my mother didn't seem interrupted enough to look for him. My grandparents moved into a house only ten minutes away, my grandfather retiring early: he became an unobvious stay-at-home father whom Manny turned to calling dad the day the first syllable broke. There just never came a point in time for any of us to correct him. It wasn't until his funeral that my mother and I realized she possessed one son, and one sibling; that I was an only child; that Manny and I were perhaps always cousins. We were plagued with wrong definitions.

At the square's center, there's a sizable group of people standing in a half-moon around the gazebo. Their focus is a woman with deep, black hair two steps up, her head tilted back and projecting. As I edge closer, I realize it's a tour, as she spits out one state fact after another, from the yucca flower to the greater roadrunner, all with rote, dismissive pleasure, before moving onto the broader points of discussion:

"My people are Acoma," she says, her hands feeling her heart. "The Acoma are one of the few tribes to still occupy pueblo villages that were home to their ancestry."

"How tall's a roadrunner?" someone asks.

"Little," she says hurriedly. "Each year, the Acoma recommit to the pueblos, not in an act of pilgrimage, but with the same purpose and reverence that provided for our kin."

"Are they easy to find?" the same voice follows up, presumably about the roadrunners.

"All over," the woman says, with a flick of her wrist. In turning their heads away from her, the group begins to spy handfuls of road-runners as they smart to and fro, kicking aloft the clay with little punches from their feet.

"The pueblo to which we call home still rests on the same mesa, over thirty stories high."

"Is it near Abiquiu?" a new voice asks, and several heads turn with interest.

"No," the woman answers. "It's nowhere near Abiquiu," and descends the gazebo, leading the group away from the square, defeated.

A few stragglers huddle away from the crowd, including the

man who had last asked a question. Off whatever impulse, I come between their group.

"Excuse me," I say. "What's in Abiquiu?"

"Uh-bee-kwu," he says.

"Sorry, Abiquiu," I repeat. "What's there?"

"The flower lady," the man says. "That's where she lived. Christ, what's her name?"

"Georgia O'Keeffe," his wife says.

"Georgia O'Keeffe," he repeats on her heels.

"Oh," I say. "People really seem to love her here."

"You don't?" the man says verging annoyed, but doesn't wait for an answer, ambling off with his wife in tow, who tugs his arm toward a card table of hammered jewelry.

An hour more, and I'm ready to give up carrying the rug. Santa Fe is small, but, with the yearly intake of tourists, is filled with hotels. I find one opposite a block of art galleries that's an entire pueblo recreation with largely lit terraces, fawning up-lights, and wooden ladders leading in and out of Shakespearean windowsills. Somehow, the hotel is more affordable than any hotel I can think of back in Nashville.

"What brings you to Santa Fe?" the attendant checking me in asks.

"My grandfather," I say.

"Does he live in town?"

"No, he passed away recently, but he talked a lot about New Mexico."

"You're here to scatter ashes!" she says cheerily, clicking away on her keyboard.

"He was buried, actually."

"Shame. The desert's a beautiful place to scatter ashes."

I nod, realizing that sounds true. Even the word scatter, to be dispersed, particulate and windswept; it suggests an immaterial finish. I wasn't even paying attention to the direction the casket faced during the memorial. I don't even know which way his feet point.

"That's one room, two double beds, check out at eleven tomorrow. Oh, I forgot to ask, would you like your room to be near the other Miranda?"

"What other Miranda?"

"A Mr. Manuel? He checked in an hour ago, also from Wisconsin …I just assumed—"

"I'm sorry," I say, and hold up a hand. Manuel, I think. I don't even recognize the sound of his name outside the curlicue diminutive. "Could you call that room, actually?" and the concierge dials out the extension, passing it along when it begins to ring.

"Hello?"

"Manny," I say, though it comes out with inflection.

"Bernie? Jesus. Did mom tell you to check in on me? I've literally been out of the state for all of four hours."

"Mom knows you're here?"

"Of course! You got her all freaked out in the car, when she realized I've never left the state either. She practically forced the plane ticket on me."

"And you picked Santa Fe?"

"It was all I could think of. I thought, fuck it, I'll go look for more clues—Wait, what do you mean here?"

Manny's room is on the highest floor, and has views that point toward the square, though isn't high enough to actually overlook.

He has a king bed with a backpack tossed on it, the minibar already exposed. His hair is wet and matted down into bangs, with his towel wrapped around his neck like a horseshoe. Instantly, I recall our childhood, and the twice-daily showers Manny used to insist upon, always working to improve some angle of his health, under the constant impression he was born jeopardized.

"So you came around to the idea?" he says.

"No," I say, "I honestly don't know why I flew out here." Shuffling around the room, I drop my bags on a corner of the bed. "There's literally hundreds of Felix Mirandas. I'm not sure how your idea made any sense."

"We'll see. City hall opens at eight on Monday," he says, to which I have no response, this odd inkling of pride creeping over me like a fog.

"What's that?" Manny asks, pointing to the rug, and I push it his way.

"Can I open it?" he asks, but doesn't wait for my reply, carefully untying the ribbons and rolling back the paper in motion with the rug.

"Jesus," he says. "What an ugly fucking rug."

"I know," I say.

"How much was it?"

"Two-seventy-five."

"Seriously? You paid $300 for this little rug?"

"It all happened quickly. I thought I'd send it to mom."

"What's she going to do with an ugly rug?" Manny demands.

"Want to get out of this room? I could use a drink that's not miniature," I say.

"Sure. Though, I have plans already."

⊙

The Georgia O'Keeffe Museum sits unassumingly outside the downtown square, a slice of modern architecture slipped neatly between two rock-faced insurance agencies. Winter, yes, but a steady outflow of visitors is visible even as we approach. It's also fifteen dollars a head.

"What a rip," Manny says. "You close in thirty minutes. Do you prorate?"

"For sixty, you can become a member, and that comes with a free guest pass."

"It says here that Santa Fe residents only cost forty-five," Manny says, pointing to a sign on the desk, as if the receptionist would be unaware.

"Do you live in town?" she asks.

"No, but our grandfather used to. We're here trying to find out about his past. Does that get us anything, like a family discount?" he asks, and the woman smiles.

"One resident membership for two cute grandsons," she says, and Manny smiles big, indicating for me to pay.

"You live in Wisconsin?" she says, handing back my license and credit card.

"Just born there," I say, and the woman puts her hand on my wrist.

"Georgia was born in Wisconsin."

"I didn't know," I say.

"Well of course you didn't know—that's how kismet works."

The museum is clean and white, a blank-check environment unfurled in every direction, with those patented leather benches and the costume-sized buttons the centerpiece of each room. In other words, it's every museum. However, for the end of a day outside tourist season, it's still crowded, legs and murmurs aswarm.

"It's packed," Manny says. "Are these locals?"

"No idea," I say.

The rooms are laid out chronologically: here's a picture Georgia made at age five for her mother's refrigerator; here's a still life Georgia's college professor told her wasn't any good; here's a scrap of charcoal shapes someone dug out of Georgia's wastebin when she wasn't looking; and, finally, here is Georgia O'Keeffe, resident mutineer of convention.

The latter series is the mainstay of the museum, with every flower painting you've either seen before or strangely recognize, all occupied by the pyramidal forms of onlookers. Each corresponding placard goes on to describe the flowers' clefts and innuendo.

"To think," Manny says, "she spent fifty years explaining to men that they weren't vaginas, only to arrive to an era when women needed them to be vaginas."

"I don't think I know as much about Georgia as people would like," I say.

"Didn't you have Ms. Prokes for art?"

"Sure."

"She was obsessed. That whole room was covered in prints."

"It was?"

"She had that giant one behind her desk. It was a cross, zoomed in really close. The painting is basically all black except for this little sliver of sunset. Remember?" he says, which I thinly recollect, or my brain conjures up a make-believe image for me to go from.

"That was a long time ago."

Manny pushes me to the side in a hurry, and I see his arm reach across the gallery floor and find the woman who checked us in.

"Excuse me. The painting with the large black cross, and the little line of sunset, do you know it?"

"Of course," she says.

"Is that one here?"

"I'm afraid not. Though, if you're interested, members can request art shares with the museum. If you put one in today, you might be able to see it here the summer after next."

"Wow, only two summers," I say.

"Don't listen to him. How do we put in the request?" Manny asks.

"Well, if two summers is too long, maybe you'd like to visit where she was when she painted it?"

"Let me guess, Abiquiu?" I ask.

"Yes! Well—Ah-bi-que," she corrects.

From the airport in Albuquerque, Manny had rented a small Kia Rio, and paid for full features: satellite radio, roadside assistance, a window-mounted GPS, even insured it for up to two million dollars in damages. On Sunday morning, I'm looking over the receipt after loading my luggage into the backseat. The plan being to drive to Georgia's property, take a picture, and head back for the airport, where I would take the only direct flight home.

"Why'd you pay for all this extra stuff?" I say looking over the sheet.

"Mom reserved it, you know her," he says, fiddling with the GPS. "Okay, what are the coordinates?" he says.

"Just type Abiquiu."

"Coordinates are more romantic, more thrill-seeking. Can't you get them from the map she gave us?"

I unfold the map from the gift shop, and trace my eyes around the route. A goofy dotted treasure line in permanent marker smudged against the laminate creases. On it, cartoon imagery simplify each town: a bottle of sarsaparilla in Albuquerque, a plated burrito in Taos, an adobe chapel in Los Cruces. Abiquiu is absent of markers.

"It doesn't have coordinates. We just drive north and it's on the left," I say.

"What is this world coming to," he says, and shifts out of park.

The drive is flat and treeless: long bridges of rock slink by at a distance, while the foreground remains patterned with low, desiccated plants. At one point, we open a game of desert I Spy when we see a real-life tumbleweed, but no other clichés surface. The night before, I had searched out the painting on my phone at Manny's request. It's just as Manny described, but beneath the arms of the cross are rows of hummocks, or sand dunes. They ripple outward in the painting, like the bottoms of egg cartons. As far as we can see, however, there are no hills like these in New Mexico.

"*Cactaceae: A Comprehensive Guide to the Great American Cactus?*" Manny says, rummaging around in my bag.

"I bought it at the airport."

Manny begins to flipbook the pages, and I regret immediately agreeing to switch drivers at every gas stop.

"'A columnar cactus generally does not flower until 35 years of age, and branches may not appear until the ages of 50 to 70 years; though many may not grow fruitful arms until 100 years. The average life span of an adult columnar is between 150 and 175 years. However, some biologists reason that varieties can live beyond 200 years.' Was this book $300, too?"

"I thought there'd be more cactuses here. Tall ones," I say.

"Saguaro," Manny says.

"How does everyone know that?"

He shrugs and, from his pocket, pulls out a small plastic device that looks like a pennywhistle. He raises it to his lips like a keepsake, and then puts it back away.

"What's that?"

"My inhaler."

"What happened to your old inhaler?"

"Gas inhalers don't push medicine into the lungs any faster than these. It's quiet. Sexier," he says with a pause. "Cheaper, mostly."

The night before, as I lay in the king bed next to Manny, his CPAP machine divided us. In the years since we last shared a room, this device had also been made sexier, barely registering a noise, its tubing outlet no longer an oxygen mask, but a snorkel that suctioned against Manny's nose. In seeing it, another memory released, from when I was eight and Manny barely two, our father having just left for another tour. I remembered, in the middle of the night, going to Manny's barely-a-bed, the thrum of that old machine kicking on and off like an accordion. I saw it as the reason he kept leaving, the reason we never slept.

I pulled off the breathing mask, the elastic quickly untucked from his tiny head. I put it next to him, right beside his pillow, and even though the machine was still running, it was like hearing the world anew. Maybe if it stayed off this one time, Manny wouldn't need it again. Maybe if it stayed off, he'd come home, wrap his arms around us. Maybe if it stayed off, we wouldn't need Manny at all.

I don't know whether or not I was going to put it back on, but from the doorway our grandfather emerged. He returned the mask to Manny's face, delicately looping it over his ears, and pointed me back to bed. He never said a word about what I'd done, or considered I'd take it off again. Though, lying in bed last night, the soundlessness of the machine's pulse, I wasn't thinking about why my grandfather never said anything, I wasn't even thinking about how he came to be standing at the door. All I thought was what it was like to hold his hand that final time, the oxygen mask pinched over his nose—did he hold my hand and remember what I had done?

"We're here," Manny says.

"Already?"

"You turned autopilot as soon as I started reading your cactus dictionary," he says, pointing us toward an overlook.

Manny gets out of the car and stretches. He looks in both directions, and then over to me. He doesn't say anything, just scratches at the back of his head. A small hike away, in Manny's background, is a pueblo outhouse. Windowless, vacant, it's roughly molded together like a tomb. In front of it are three wooden crosses that front a rocky declivity.

"That," Manny points, and he begins to lead us forward. However, at a few hundred feet off, it's clear this looks nothing like the painting. The crosses aren't even set facing west, but south, so that no line of horizon would even be visible. Likewise, the hills are not hills, but patches of shrub and feather grass.

Near enough, Manny plants his hand on the middle cross.

"No way this is it," he says.

"What other cross could it be?"

"There has to be somewhere else."

I turn around, pretending to dizzy myself, but am fine giving in.

"I think this is it," I say.

"You are just about the worst brother detective there is," he says. "You don't want to find our grandfather's secret life, you don't want to find Georgia O'Keeffe's cross. You can't even find a tall cactus."

"In my defense, I only came looking for the cactus."

From behind Manny, a dozen people surface from a small, wizened ledge of rock. Their heads peculiar blurs of life. They peer over the outlook, and then disappear.

"What about up there?" I ask, and Manny turns just as the group withdraws.

"Up there?" he repeats, and I push us forward across a craggy footpath, which eventually links to a set of stairs made from railroad ties, marching us into the sun.

At the top, dozens of tourists, all bundled up, are spaced across the property. The center of their shared interest is a ranch home, with perfectly massaged right angles, and wall-wide windows. Immediately it's clear that this is Georgia's home. Or was.

Between the herds of onlookers, docents scurry them in and out of rooms, survey her gardens, her favorite resting spots. Each group that passes seems more enamored than the previous. Manny pulls out his inhaler and takes two more breaths at the top, leading us momentarily into a tour group, before breaking away toward the house's front door, his arm tugging on my jacket.

"I think we're supposed to pay," I say, looking for a kiosk.

"Are you kidding? We're members," and Manny leads us in.

The possessions we find are all cold and indirect. Flat chairs, flat tables, no rugs. It's a home that's never been cozied, and maintains the desired world of her paintings—almost too purposefully. Possibly this was how she lived, but more likely everything persists how someone else envisioned a person to be. Someone without a toothbrush cup, or ringlets of stained water at their bedside. Someone who didn't grow frustrated, or draw lousily, or even splatter food when she cooked. Someone who just woke up and painted the sunset, the flowers, the crosses, and lived every day as an elegy.

I look over to Manny who is standing beside her bed, which sits exposed in the main room. He motions secretly for me, but there's no one else in this part of the house.

"What?" I say, reaching him, and he points to the bed.

"Lie down," he says. "I'll take our picture."

"In the bed?" I ask, but Manny is already glancing around in a huff, and getting himself situated, trying not to press any dirt from his boots onto the coverlet.

"Come on," he says. "One picture, we'll be up and out." I look around the room, and through the corner windows can see out onto the courtyards and swimming pool, where visitors visor their eyes to better see the views, to playact what she saw.

"One picture," he repeats.

The two of us crunch together in a bed half the size of the hotel's, our shoulders pressed like logs. Manny pulls his phone from his pocket, and positions it above our heads. At first it faces the ceiling, but he flips the camera around, so that we can see ourselves in its screen. The camera autofocuses us in place; it centers our features, and holds them there for a moment, where we both pull back the same smile.

"Count of three," he says, but immediately takes the picture.

When Georgia O'Keeffe first arrived in New Mexico, she couldn't find any flowers. Amid the dunes and rock cover, she claimed all she found were bones. Barrels worth of horse and cow heads, skeletons too eroded to puzzle back together. Each morning, she'd walk a different vector of earth, trying not to repeat the same line. Sometimes she could carry only a single vertebra. Other times, she amassed gentle armfuls of remains. Back at her house, she'd pile them out front, a mound slowly linking together as more arrived.

Years later, just ahead of her 90th birthday, she gave a series of interviews for PBS. About the bones, she said, "It never occurs to me that they have anything to do with death."

"They are very lively," she said.

Three hours later, and I'm sitting in the departures terminal, one rug rolled up and slipped under the main flap of my backpack like a small sleeping bag, when Manny texts me.

Not thirty minutes earlier he'd dropped me off out front, goofily smiling in my direction, like I was somehow a child he was releasing back into the world.

"Well," he said, "Sorry we didn't get any cactus pictures."

"That's okay," I said. "Driving straight back?"

"I don't know. Mom booked the hotel room for a week. In that time I could probably see every city in this state."

"Maybe you can find the cross she was looking at," I said, which Manny didn't respond to right away, before opening his eyes to agree he might.

"You okay?" I asked, which, harmless enough, was not a question I was prone to asking.

"What do I do if it's him," he said. "Even if I find an address, it won't tell me anything."

"Maybe you're just supposed to look," I said. "I flew out here too."

"Yeah, but to see some really old cactus," he said, which I couldn't totally disagree with in the moment. Though, wading through the terminal, I realized I'd flown here for my grandfather, yes, but also for my grandmother, for Manny, for an entire family of reasons I could neither parcel out nor hold all at once.

Sliding open my phone, I see Manny has texted me:

"There. Proof we were both here," along with the picture of us in Georgia's supposed bed, which can barely be seen, which has no historic marker or significance, and could just as well be the bed of a stranger some thousand miles away. I move my thumbs across the image and zoom in against our faces. Only, the more I look at the picture, the more I see my grandfather's face in ours, as if aged in reverse and brought into the future. It's saying the same thing it did the last time I saw him, his hand pushing into mine: you fight you fight you fight.

Scenario

O ne of the pranks we play on our daughter is called
Watershed. Truthfully, it's less a prank and more hide-
and-seek for the grown-up imagination, or perhaps emergency preparedness for the child imagination. Who's to say, though,
because the second Amelia was born it was like age was a concept
we folded up neatly and dumped into a suitcase in the hall closet.
Age doesn't have bearing on survival the same way traumas that are
natural or manufactured don't have any consideration for existence.
What does a hurricane need the sunset for? In terms of its lifespan,
fleeting and impulsive, there's simply no time to sit and see a thing.
So, no, Amelia isn't any age, and we're not any age, and disaster is
never caught off-guard by the sight of the moon. All this to say, puer-
ile or prescient notwithstanding, in our house, we play Watershed.

The goal of the game is twofold: navigate from Point A to Point B, and do not be seen, and it was brought to us by a community center workshop called "It Could Happen to You." Like that old movie, whose plot I can't totally remember. "It Could Happen to You" was advertised pretty heavily for several weeks leading up to its weekend set of sessions, the cost of which was made free and open to the public.

The co-hosts of the sessions were two former emergency response officers reputed to have been everywhere, from mine fallouts to active shooters to the standing waters in the Gulf we know all too well: Barney and Maxine, polar opposites in approach and physique. Barney was lanky and tender, glasses as tight as goggles; he was borderline praying mantis. While Maxine was considerably more filled out in ways you could feel confidence about: a mop of brown chainlink trusses atop a jukebox of muscle, but she smiled endlessly.

Together, they had chiseled out a routine that worked its way from library basements to city halls, all in the name of what public safety could look like. In uncertain terms, they were less fear-mongers and more safety-mongers, unless those turn out to be the same.

Ahead of the workshop, Court and I sat in bed watching old YouTube videos of the pair, which were mostly testimonials, where tearing family members recounted how their instincts targeted in the sessions had been completely remade, pulverized and polished. From the queue came enumerations as far-reaching as preventing the spread of campfires, thwarting rabid animals, sidestepping gas station hold-ups—even some quick thinking during a PG-13 sexcapade from two paled parents.

"Fight or flight is the most identifiable concept for people in the crosshairs of a situation," says Max during the talking head of one video. From stage right, Barney enters the frame and the camera pulls back: "Let us teach you how to monopolize that instinct and not rely on panic to make your decisions."

Court paused there on the laptop.

"What do you think?" she asked. "Too paranoid?"

"I don't know," I said. "It doesn't seem like something we'd have done before Amelia."

"Obviously. But we're sort of in a new era."

"It's not a new era. It was a singular event, a freak moment. Not an era."

Court rolled her eyes at my attempt to pacify, and therefore belittle, the fact that two weeks before the workshop flyers started showing up on car windows, two weeks before the Hesses and the Flemings called to tell us they'd already signed up for the classes—two weeks before all of that—a letter was sent home from Amelia's school explaining a student, not to be named but whose name we all immediately discovered, had brought an unloaded firearm to school. "No ammunition, the safety on," the letter said, an attempt to frame how little risk it posed. Only, we knew the safety could be released, we understood that ammunition could be loaded in, the same way we could fill a high schooler with vodka sodas and send their cars in the direction of our enemies. No matter how we classified it, it cut us all the same length.

Court looked back to the screen and hit play, a quick crossfade to a woman sitting on her front porch with a young boy, maybe 10 or 12. The woman is clearly the mother, and the boy has his eyes trained into the porch boards.

"It was a year ago last month," she begins. "Todd here had been at karate. I'd just dropped him off and was headed back home, when our neighbor called to tell me about it. I was still around the corner, but as soon as I looked out the window I could see the smoke." The woman blinks hard, and recovers.

"I knew my husband had gotten up that morning wanting to make a big breakfast. And Adam, our youngest, was going to help out. My husband went to check on the dryer in the basement, which had been making a loud noise the past few days. The basement door was right off the kitchen, and when he opened it—or what they believe happened—is when he opened it, gas that had been leaking was freed into the house. Adam lit the burner on the stove, and it all—" she says, pausing with a harder wince than before, while Todd's hand awkwardly consoles her shoulder. Court and I both sat upright, realizing the testimonial might actually go a bit further than suggested.

"Adam wasn't knocked out. He went for the living room, and found a blanket on the couch and pulled it over himself. He crawled like that all the way to the front door, and made it into the yard." The mother completes her sentence, but catches again, and this time Todd aims his face away where the small veins of his forehead rush out in anguish.

"My husband recovered, but Adam…he inhaled too much smoke," she says. "He didn't make it, but he knew what to do. He did just like we practiced, and all I can think now is, thanks to these classes, Adam gave himself a chan—"

I hit pause.

"Fuck," Courtney said.

"Fuck," I repeated, and the images poured over us. If a workshop designed to help save lives couldn't even save lives, we thought, then surely no workshop at all was, not tempting fate, but providing it a roadmap.

⊙

Simply stated, the Point B in Watershed represents safety, or its closest approximation. Many times Point B is the shed in the backyard, a tire swing at the park around the corner, which has been Amelia's stomping ground since bipedalism arrived.

Point A, on the other hand, is a living variable. This is the origin of danger, the unpredictable, which makes it our responsibility to chart and path the radius of Amelia's life to keep the origin current: trips to the bank with her grandmother; the few minutes a day of outdoor fun, where we watch her anxiously from the kitchen window; the Mezzanine Street Bridge, which is probably the most formidable bridge in the whole state, except for the fact that it crosses the Mississippi and is a suspension bridge, meaning our car during rush hour is just a trapeze artist out there in one of those daring free-falls with wrists extended hoping someone strong enough is on the other end—so yes, fuck yes even, we made the Mezzanine Street Bridge and its legendary sturdiness a Point A.

Other conditions of the game are a bit more restrained. Barney and Maxine advised using obstacles and instruments in the boundaries of everyday use: a straw can be a snorkel, a pocket bible can stop an arrow. In light of this, we appealed the game to Amelia by allowing her more freedoms. From longer ventures away from the house to using the scissors we keep in the high cupboards—essentially, within the construct of the game, she is exempt of limitation. If she figures out how to drive the car with a pogo stick, the only consequence is our admiration.

To accommodate our schedule, we signed up for the Saturday session, nine to one. A four-hour crash course seemingly intent on moving our parental needles from latchkey to panic room. Court's mom stopped over to watch Amelia, providing us sideline commentary as we dug around for spare notebooks and pens that wouldn't bleed out mid-scribble.

"I just thought you two had your way, or your instincts already," she said.

"That's exactly what worries us," Court explained. "What do we know about instincts neither of us have ever used?"

Her mom just shrugged and turned from the kitchen to the playroom, where all forty pounds of Amelia sat at her worktable divvying up play-doh with a dinosaur cookie-cutter. That morning, Amelia had woken us both with a particularly thrilled expression, jumping across the coverlet with these cookie-cutters, which we couldn't even remember buying. From there, she instructed us to help her squeeze into last year's Halloween costume, a Princess and the Frog theme she had long outgrown: bottom half frog, top half princess. A few balletic numbers down the stairs, and she was pulling ingredients from the cupboards.

For so long, Amelia has existed in this exact format of unambiguous delight. During the initial months, a midnight cough, or a sharp corner at eye level, held such power and threat over our daily lives. However, the more often she was sick, the more faceplants she took into the kitchen tile, the stronger our immune systems became. We acclimated as parents, discovered trust in the universe, but the day we signed up for the workshops we were reminded of her survival— of what unrelenting effort it takes to actually secure your child's life.

If there were ever a chance for us to rescue her from the unforeseeable, it would be now, when each day was a private quest to equip herself with more, a new brain fighting off a new body that would soon become a potato sack of hormones bent on succumbing her to every judgment of the world. If we could just lower her into that depth with a steadier hand, maybe she could remain ageless a while longer.

The community center has held many iterations, but its latest turn was a giant multi-purpose room with enough linoleum to commit to anything. Filing in, we recognized a few parents from Amelia's class—some we knew by name, others by face, but it gave the impression we weren't the only ones kept awake thinking about the Adams of the world.

Barney and Maxine were standing in front, in matching olive polos and black, waterproof pants with pockets overrunning. Each was midway through a bottle of water, and laughing between sips with another man dressed like a volunteer firefighter.

At five to nine, Max separated she and Barn from conversation, and the volunteer went for the doors, pulling them shut and killing the lights. As he did, Barney moved window to window pulling down large blackout screens that ate up the daylight, one by one, like sealing in floorboards. A few people began to pull out their phones to finish conversations.

"At this time, all phones must be off," Max said, and without question, the chirps of powering down patterned around the audience.

I leaned to whisper to Court, but she placed her hand over her ear to block me.

It was Court who first told me about the workshop, which I originally dismissed as reactionary. A trauma-based money-maker, I believe I'd said. However, once I saw there was real fear to her thoughts, the same fears found their way under my skin; they kept reminding me how few times I'd actually had to account for Amelia's life, or Court's for that matter. Her hand over her ear was a distinct reminder not to fall on old ways: what has criticism ever protected?

The sound of footsteps organized at the front, and we presumably crossed the nine o'clock hour.

"SCENARIO!" Maxine yelled out, startling a dozen chair legs to attention, before Barney cut quickly in: "An intruder has entered your house through a ground floor window. You and your loved one are asleep upstairs. You hear a window break, but they do not. Your son's room is downstairs. What's the first thing you do?"

"Wake my husband," a woman called out.

"Good," Barn said. "The two of you are awake. What's next?"

"Call the police," someone said.

"Sure, sure. But what does that mean? Whispering to the dispatcher, giving information, then waiting for them to arrive. What if you live in a part of town police don't care about?" Though no one answered or affirmed his question. "What else?"

"Go downstairs," someone said.

"How?"

"Quietly, my phone in my hand with 9-1-1 dialed."

"Alright," he relented. "Let's try that. The two of you make it downstairs. Your child's bedroom is in the front of the house. What next?"

"Save yourselves, get to the car!" someone joked.

"Look for the broken window!" another shouted.

"Why?"

"Maybe you can track the guy," the same voice said.

"Great. You fight?" Again, no one answered.

"I'm serious, how many people here fight regularly?"

"Time!" Maxine yelled. "Sixty seconds and no plan."

"SCENARIO!" Barney shouted, and the volunteer flipped on the light blinding us all in reverse, and Maxine took over.

"You arrive home late at night, and immediately see no lights are on in your house. This is unusual. Your teenage child is supposed to be home. You're a single parent. You park in the garage, and discover the door to your house pried open. What do you do?"

"Snoop through their stuff!" called a voice.

"Why's that?" Max asked.

"Clues, maybe some weed to smoke?" the voice replied, and a few parents snickered.

"Let's focus," Max said. "What do you do?"

"Turn on the lights."

"Good. Though I'm guessing that's a lot of light switches, maybe a lot of lamps."

"Grab a flashlight?"

"No, the light on your phone," another person insisted.

"Okay, get that on, and enter the house. Your child's room is upstairs. Where do you go first?"

"The kitchen. Get a knife."

"Weaponry, yes. Everyone feels better with a weapon. Let's go one further. You have guns in the garage. Want to get those?" The audience released a noise of approval, and Court turned skeptically to face me.

"You," Maxine called in our direction, and Court bolted her head forward.

"You don't have guns?" she asked, and Court shook her head.

"Let's say you do, do you want to pick them up now?" Courtney paused, as if to first embody a gun-owner, delineate her rights, and then, uncertainly, said:

"I don't kn—"

"Time!" Barney shouted, and the light elapsed.

The next two hours continued with scenarios playing out more and more rapidly, most of us simply listening, privately debating what we would do differently, too meek to reveal our voices. Of course, as time tracked on, it was clear this design was effective. It was clear our audience was picking up on how easily we steered into corners of desperate thinking. And yet, at the same time, Barney and Maxine were selling us reassurance. Shiny, concretized reassurance that maybe we didn't know what we were doing this morning, but by this afternoon, our families would never be at risk again.

"Scenario," Max said at a normal volume, finding her way alongside Barney.

"You're at home in the middle of the day," he said. "Your child's in the backyard. There's a knock on the door, a delivery person. You answer it and sign for a package, no more than a minute. When you return to the kitchen, you find your child is lying on the ground unconscious. Approach the situation."

"Check to see if they're breathing."

"They're breathing," Barney said.

"Are they discolored?"

"Slightly pale."

"Call an ambulance."

"Call an ambulance," Barney repeated.

"Time," Max said, and released a shade behind her to reveal daylight, the beams fanning across our faces, the two co-hosts radiating at the front like saviors.

"There are days when the world simply takes over," Maxine picked up, as if straight from their videos. "We're not here to prevent danger. These trainings are meant to improve your response to danger."

"In our opening scenarios, everyone acted thoughtfully, but there were a lot of missteps," Barney admitted, and Max raised her arms in the air, two fists large enough to drag in a plane.

"Sneaking around the house in the dark," Max said putting up a finger. "Taking weapons to an unknown situation around loved ones. Eyes on the danger, and not on what you need to protect," and slowly Max's fingers filled out like antlers, each imagined nib of bone our failures.

"Now," Barney said. "I'd like everyone to pick up their chairs and make a large circle. We're going to use our remaining time to learn a game that will let us rethink our approaches. Even better, this will be a game you can play with your family."

On our way home, Courtney and I were both invigorated. In several hours time we'd gone from taking on uncertain cues to having immediate direction for how to assess a situation. Out our windows, everything held such crisped form. We drove back to the house calling out scenarios, becoming desperately and ridiculously held to the game, always in explicit agreement with the other's approach.

"You're out to dinner when a man enters with a gun. You're sitting next to Amelia in a booth. What's next?" I asked.

"I push Amelia beneath the table and I walk for the door. The gunman follows me rather than checking the booth."

"Good," I said, and a small, elemental part of me fully meant '*good.*' I want a wife who's so much stronger than a gun, who is so much stronger than death. My wife is dead, because she has to be.

Barney and Maxine recommended the game begin at home, in a

setting we might take for granted as safe and invulnerable. In doing so, Amelia might reveal how she navigated our home, alerting us to what she doesn't understand about the adult world at her disposal. After a few rounds, we were encouraged to take the game off-campus to restaurants, friends' houses; the more public the theater the better. The only additional prerequisite was to develop the arc of the game ahead of time and keep task in a notebook, to not simply repeat the more obvious disasters.

In preparation for the first round, Court and I stayed up practically the whole night, elaborating on all matter of circumstance, until we reached those hinterlands of make-believe and ruin. The premier game occurred the weekend after with a light instructional breakfast.

"To start, you'll get back in bed, and we'll pretend you've just woken up like any other day, only we're not home. Now, we won't go far, but we won't be here to help you. After ten minutes, I want you to get out of bed, look around the house, and get to one of the safe zones we talked about. Do you remember our safe zones?"

On the other side of the counter, Amelia stabbed into a defrosted waffle, the sound of her socks rubbing together.

"Out by the shed, the park, under the bed in the guest room."

"Exactly," Court said. "Those are all good places."

"Ready?" I asked, and she put down her fork and slouched off the barstool.

In her room, we arranged her under the covers. We kissed her forehead, explained again and again how this was all for our safety, so that we'd always be together, and we left the room.

Court and I immediately began to upset all ends of the house as planned: drawers opened, table lamps artfully scattered to the ground, we yanked out the phone cords, unplugged the internet; we turned on the kitchen faucet, opened the oven door, flipped couch cushions; and more and more ideas sniffed us out until the house was generally purposed into mania.

We looked around and found absolute approval in what we'd done, and pointed each other out of the house, scampering across the backyard for the shed. We reasoned the shed was exactly where Amelia would end up. After seeing the house, there was no way she would head back upstairs, and on such a clouded day, she wasn't going to the park just to get rained on.

"Are we supposed to time her?" Court asked, but I shook my head. On a first run, we didn't need to think about that. This wasn't sport, but survival.

Outside, a small break of sound clipped the shingles, until it found a familiar rhythm. The rain grew and settled around us, almost enjoyably, and Courtney and I exchanged a look of confidence that such phenomena would point our daughter back to us.

However, ten minutes is hardly a measure of time—seconds, really. And so when those seconds passed and there was still no sign of her, it wasn't yet cause for concern, no prehensile fears to allay. She was simply a young mind in a new surrounding.

"How long has it been?" Court asked.

"Thirteen minutes," I said, though still not pressured.

"Something feels wrong," Courtney said.

"It's supposed to make us uncomfortable," I reminded. "How are we going to leave her alone if we don't know she can handle herself?"

"She's five. We aren't going to leave her alone."

"Five more minutes," I said, and Court moved away from me, cracking the door to peer out, where the rain continued to thread the air.

I understood it was a risk we were taking with Amelia, I did, but it was a controlled risk: safety by design. It was the sort of attempt our parents never took with us, and so the kind of attempt we must take with ours.

Still, as twenty minutes rolled up, I could feel Courtney inflate the room with panic, a phrase of hatred and remorse pulling her face toward opposite ends, and she pushed open the door, trudging for the house, where I could only assume Amelia was camped between the couch cushions watching a show. Yet, when I followed out the shed, I found it too, that same admixture of regret and disgust blurring Court formed over me, a cheap eggshell of potential doom.

My legs picked up, and I entered the house, which was still perfectly suspended in disorder. Only Amelia wasn't in the living room, the TV was off, and as I shuffled between the first-floor rooms, my shoes squeaking from the rain, she wasn't in the kitchen, the dining area, anywhere. Courtney flowed down the stairs.

"She's not under the bed," she said, and we both knew exactly what this meant: our daughter, the butterfly collector, the insect magnet, went undeterred through the rains to Safe Zone 3. I ran for the backyard, and Court went for the front, each way leading to the same park yet different entrances, our newly combined instincts understanding we must cover all bases.

Though it's not the most practical route, the park can be reached through the alleys of others' backyards, like a private corridor of unmown meadow, which Amelia and I often traversed, her knobby legs pinching over top my shoulders, me playacting a giant. Clearing the high grass, it scraped at my pants, as if to claw me on purpose.

Entering in, I was immediately swept up in the park's history, how for so long it had been the keeper of the most pressing memories of Amelia we owned. It was where she stumbled out her first steps, where a bee sting swelled into a golf ball and nearly ended our marriage, even the site of a quietly powerful moment of sexual recovery the first night we entrusted Amelia to a babysitter. Yet, in the center of all its green, she was not. Not twirling in the open, not kicking midair at the swing set, not transforming the fallen branches into sword points.

From the opposite direction, Courtney came bounding in, her legs moving from excited to collapsible, as she bent in half. She stood upright and looked in my direction several hundred feet off. She threw her arms in frustration, and turned back for the house; only, something kept me. A mode of destruction I knew I wouldn't be able to articulate to Courtney later on when all this was behind us, when Amelia was safe and sound, and we were settling in for bed. She'd stand there looking for me to explain how I could have simply stayed. But, despite our training, a part of me still clung to the fact that Amelia's survival must rely on the instincts she's received from both of us. If my instinct was to press deeper into the park, then it may have been Amelia's to do exactly the same, to move against logic.

Even still, I couldn't help but think back to Adam, to the little hilltops of bone soldiering forward, the smell of his breath trapped in place. Seeing how easily the failures can find you, I could almost feel the warmth of him: his friction across the rooms, the black outflows of smoke eating through the holes of the blanket, bringing it all to a cellular, atomic end.

Photophobia

At the eye doctor, I realize I have not been to the eye doctor in nearly two years. Partly because of the pandemic, partly the online optometry service where one can be issued a new prescription for eyeglasses and contacts simply by taking a picture of their eyes, but the last time I was at the eye doctor was for a cornea ulcer. The occasion landed me in a grueling session of eye drops every thirty minutes for a day and a half, so that I had to set my alarm through the night for exactly this metronome of responsibility and in predawn hours debated whether I would survive kids. Now interested in becoming a parent, I wonder if this call for a much bigger responsibility is why I've returned.

"Your prescription's worsened some," she says.

"How much some?"

"Are you having trouble seeing road signs or words on your television?" she asks, which I have, yes to both, and I keep wondering if white letters on Kermit-green are the way cities should be going.

"Not really," I say, because I don't want a new prescription.

"Both eyes are similarly worse," she says, and hands me a tissue to blot at my eyes.

"What's the prescription now?"

"-6.5."

Previously, the GPA of my eyes was -5.5. They achieved this mark when I was seventeen and remained unchanged until two minutes earlier, at the age of thirty-four.

"That seems sudden, or a lot," I say.

"Well, truthfully, they may have worsened years ago. It says here you haven't seen an eye doctor in over four years, since 2018, is that right? For an ulcer?"

I readdress my math.

"That's right."

"What about light sensitivity? When you're in the sun, how does that affect you?"

"Aren't my eyes supposed to improve with age, when you're near-sighted?"

"The reason I'm asking about the light sensitivity is because, based on where your eyes are, you now have to pay attention to flashes and floaters. Have you been noticing these?"

"No," I say, but I don't know what flashes are and am using context to define floaters.

"Well, we don't really go in for pamphlets anymore, so I want you to google them. They're essentially translucent or dark squiggles you can see move across your line of vision, sometimes they hang there like a cobweb. If you start to notice a lot of them, you can go to any eye doctor's office to be seen. Don't even make an appointment, just go to the closest one. They're an indicator of retinal detachment, but not always dangerous, but something you should have examined quickly."

On the way out of the office, the sun in the parking lot overtakes my pupils, still wishing-well-sized. Growing up, my prescription worsened too quickly for comfort and saw me at the doctor every six months for dilation drops, non-negotiable. The numbing drops became so routine their sensation transitioned to something enjoyable. Eventually my eyes stopped fighting back, they stayed put, and the eye doctor was the first responsibility I learned to let lapse. Squinting my way toward the car, I remember why.

In the car, I fumble out my phone but can't see the messages clearly. I stare into my hand instead, focused on the couch of my palm, awaiting the sight of the flotsam in my eyes going by, as if I might be allowed to then grasp it.

I keep hearing the double conjunction of the doctor but not always dangerous, but something you should have examined…its misuse peering in on me until it starts to make sense.

In thinking about kids, I mean adopting my own, as a single man, who works unsteadily on government contracts. Unsteadily but reliably, but still in a domain of 1099s that entail self-employment taxes and personal retirement contributions and lying on my returns about the square footage of my home office and the miles I've driven. Financial steps that don't seem to inspire the general security one would look for when placing a child for an impermanent number of years.

The want struck me at the end of a relationship, as many wants do, though the decision was born years earlier, slowly catching up to this coincidence. I had set myself aside for so long that I wasn't able to recognize what it means to have my own joy, to derive a sense of self, id and ego waning crescents at best.

However, by the time I crawled out from under all these peddled ideas of prioritizing myself and learning myself on a deeper level, it was clearer than ever that I was not made to live life for myself. In order to be myself, with the widest runway possible, I needed to bring someone else in and it was at the end of this relationship that I realized I was holding on, in some ways, to fulfill a future with children, unrealizing that this future doesn't need to involve someone you dislike.

In the car, it takes twenty minutes of exaggerated blinking before I can read my phone at an arm's length from my face. In my messages, I see Jessie has sent me a picture of something she's been working on, an illustration that feels both bright and muted; though, I can't get at its detail, and I blurrily read her text asking if this afternoon still works.

I type back the letter "Y."

Jessie is a friend of a friend of a friend who is better about reciprocating than anyone I've ever met, which brought us together at a birthday party where I drunkenly explained I was filling out adoption paperwork and how expensive it all was, and she drunkenly volunteered to create a campaign for this adoption to help cover some costs.

In the moment, I had agreed, but I fully intended to walk away from the idea, both prideful and unable to see a way in which I would ever email or post a request for money that would lead me down the many rabbit holes of unasked opinions; I could see myself, navigating this warren of advice until my ears began to bleed.

And yet, the morning after, Jessie messaged me a small sketch on a notecard, which not only looked like something I liked but even made me consider that neither of us were drunk. It was a drawing of a small blob, just an outline that looked like a fried egg without the yolk, and below it read: "Not all germs need an egg."

It was a joke I didn't get. Either it was about germ cells, about me being a man, or it was about nothing, but I could see it now, and the $3,000 non-refundable application fee underhand seemed like a price a person shouldn't have to pay.

I told Jessie I loved it, and she laughed saying I should not, but that if I was still interested, we should meet the following week, offering Wednesday, and I told her sure as long as she didn't mind that I might have to have my eyes dilated.

The week after the ulcer, I was supposed to fly to Arizona and drive to the Grand Canyon, which I hadn't visited since I was eleven. I asked the eye doctor overseeing me at the time if going was still possible; he shrugged and left the room for over thirty minutes. Eventually I wandered out, and, as if he were waiting for me all along as a test, he called over to the door for me to return and wait inside the exam room, that there had been an emergent situation, and he'd be along shortly.

Ten minutes more, he returned with sample drops, prescriptions, and the comically involved regimen. I asked what would happen if I fell asleep in the middle of the night, if several hours passed without the drops going in. He said if that happened, I could go to Arizona, but he would be nervous to send me to the Grand Canyon with only one eye.

The ulcer came and went and I waited to tell my friends about the ordeal in person, once we were already arrived, in the interest of having a story to share.

"What is an eye ulcer, exactly?" my friend asked.

"I'm not sure, sort of like a divot maybe? They think I had dust stuck on my eye and every day I put my contacts in, I trapped it in place, and it bore a deeper and deeper hole."

"Shouldn't you be wearing your glasses then?" another friend asked, who also wore glasses.

"I can't see as well with them," I said, suggesting that the sights we came to see were the kind you risk everything for. Yet, when we made it there, when I finally matched the version of what I had seen at age eleven with what I was seeing at age thirty, I realized it was just an enormous divot, a place through which particles had eroded over and over, unable to bear the glare of the sun, so that they worked their way furiously to anywhere else.

In looking back, though, I wonder if the emergency the doctor had been attending to was a retinal detachment, was me in another rotation of life having come in from the street to explain I was seeing pieces of my eye that had peeled apart and were now floating inside me.

At one of the two tables outside, Jessie is leaned over an iPad drawing, wearing baggy white overalls and an orange winter hat, a clashing ensemble for such a hot day.

"Hey," I say.

"Hey! Are you okay? Your eyes still look glazed over."

"I'm okay, but I might need to sit out of the sun," I say, both realizing this will entail looping masks back over our faces and having to speak in a tight-lipped manner.

"Of course!" she says, but rather than follow me in, she takes the metal table and begins to drag it along with her chair until it's eaten by shade.

Pulled up on her screen, she has created a slide deck of options, each more interesting than the previous. Some of them are beautifully lettered thank-you cards, others are cartoons: one of them a seedling that looks like a soybean upright, a small leaf sprout for a roof, and on the face of the bean a small door and window filled with light; below it the phrase "Adopt a home."

"These are amazing," I say. "I don't know how you made them so fast."

"You really like them already, no notes?"

"None. I don't even know how to choose."

"Don't! We'll use them all. Different amounts can get a tote or a print," she says.

I recline back in the chair to think for a moment, to process.

"They don't have to be totes…" she says, mostly joking.

"Sorry," I say. "Seeing it all just feels like coming into the open. It makes me concerned about how I'm going to answer questions of wanting to be a father, or what I'll say when women who are mothers suggest I try fostering first. Or maybe accepting money feels like an admission that I don't have what I think is enough, in which case maybe people should donate money to people with kids."

"You got all that from a lima bean?"

Jessie says she'll add the images to mock-ups and send along vendors she's worked with, while I agree to get a campaign page up and running, which means writing a narrative that will doubtlessly invite more questions and skepticism than my gut can conceive.

Still, I agree.

◉

The next week, I'm on a call with the Office of Emergency Management, who are asking how best to locate a new warming center for next winter. Memphis has experienced freezing temperatures more regularly the last few years, yet the chorus of the unexpected is always attached to its arrival, the planning always late, the resources always stalled.

We ultimately settle on a church off Poplar, but it's an obvious location, not a decision that would require an hourlong conversation of seven people, and yet this is exactly what's happened, with only four of us speaking. I tally the hour to bill, less social security taxes, and realize the call afforded me the printing of ten book-sized canvas totes.

At our meetup, Jessie explained smaller totes were now more fashionable on account of no one wanting totes any longer, both for their environmental impact and their general inundation. However, a book-sized tote, she assured, would sell and be cheaper to make.

If a fifty-dollar donor receives a tote, less the cost of shipping, it's thirty dollars to me. This sounds great, until I realize the number of people in my life who I speak to—who will actually see this—can be counted. Printing ten totes does not mean selling ten totes, so that my asking will result in five-hundred dollars from my mother (already a perennial donor of any future children), and another thousand from close friends. I am creating a social media campaign in order to cut the cost of an application in half—an amount, at the end of the day, I truthfully don't need.

I start to text Jessie that we should hit pause, but as my eyes focus on the white background of our thread an inchworm comes gliding into my eyeline as if pushed across an ice rink. And then another. And another. I turn away from my phone, blink hard, shake, and then look at the wall; my eyes feel overtaken, undersea.

⊙

This past winter, freezing temperatures were accompanied by a day-long rain. Everyone dripped faucets, canceled school, and cleaned out the water aisles at Kroger, anticipating terrible roads, internet outages. Both of these concerns came true, but the city also settled into an incredible menagerie, with ice wrapping every branch and offshoot, peerless and glassine, its sight mesmeric.

Only a half-inch of ice will increase the weight of tree limbs and power lines by a factor of ten, and a full inch had formed over every surface. For the next week, the city was handed over to gravity as the infrastructure swelled and burst, leaving three-hundred thousand people without power, crowding in with friends and relatives, over-flowing every room. This is what I imagine inside my eyes, that each specter free-floating across me is just another person relegated to a single room, bouncing off its corners like a screensaver.

The closest eye doctor is on Union and I park on a side street behind a garage. Inside, I go to reception and try to explain what's happening, that there are floaters inside my eyes and I believe I'm at risk of what's called retinal detachment, but I don't have an appointment, but I was told I don't need one.

The man at the desk thankfully treats me like what I'm saying is not unheard of and gets up to ask someone if they can see me. Within five minutes, a doctor opens the patient door and waves me along and begins to ask me questions as we make it to an examining room.

"How long have you been seeing them?"

"Just this hour."

"Are they mostly around bright light, bright walls or wherever you look?"

"I first noticed it looking at my phone," I say. "But now it feels like they're everywhere."

The doctor nods and points to take a seat. She disinfects the forehead rest, the chin rest, and invites me forward.

"Look at my ear," she says, and positions her head so that only one ear is in view.

"I usually see Dr. Tucker," I say, which isn't even true, and also would not be someone she necessarily knows. Though, as I think on it, I remember as a kid my orthodontist and dentist played a weekly game of tennis, so my precedent is not unfounded.

"OK," she says, backing away and turning on the lights from a control panel on the desk. "You said you first noticed this on your phone?"

I nod.

"I see no sign of detachment. More than likely you have always had these floaters, but now that you've become aware of them…"

"I notice them."

"Exactly," she says. "Floaters don't leave—where would they go? However, they're more common in eyes with stronger prescriptions and more common with, well, age."

"So, it's fine that I see them?" I try and confirm.

"It is. Now, if they begin to occlude your vision with tiny dots or you start to experience flashes," and here she blinks her hand open and shut like tossing sand in my face, "then you should do exactly as you did today, come right in. I think that's all Dr. Tucker was warning."

Again, I nod.

Jessie texts asking how the campaign writing is going, aware that I am someone prone to spiraling, but I am slow to reply, thinking how to carefully end the venture, without revealing any additional spiraling.

A retinal detachment, I read, occurs when the retinal tissue at the back of the eye has pulled away from its normal position, separating the cells living there from the blood vessels that provide it oxygen. Oftentimes, a detachment is the result of a tear in the retina that has allowed eye fluid to leak outside the vitreous, pulling the retina downward. In my mind, I see the tines of a fork push into an over-easy egg.

I also read that it's not floaters we see but their shadows cast on the retina. Our brains eventually teach us to not notice the shadows, the same way certain sounds may not leave us, but our brains immunize our ears, which at least explains why I don't always see my current lineup.

Assuming the worst, I ask the internet how to treat detachment. Each of the solutions are precisely on the line of science-fair science: injecting a bubble of air into the center of the eye to push the retina back into place and using cold therapy to repair the break; the insertion of a silicone buckle that literally wraps around the eye like a belt to take pressure away from the detachment site; but it's door number three that really holes up inside me, which is to drain the fluid in your eye completely until the vitreous refills with body fluid; I'm omitting a few crucial steps, but these are the fixes I carry forward.

In any case, there's no rhyme or reason to what vision you retain or lose with each procedure, which nullifies having to choose, meaning one day they might as well drain it, take it all out and let my body push from all directions until it's refilled, because if there's one thing I trust about the human body it's the body's fear to live with something hollow, to allow space to be space and nothing else.

Jessie sends a new text of a dozen images, her designs wrapped on drink koozies and T-shirts and laptop stickers and phone cases and coffee mugs and I realize it's too late. I am now married to circumstance.

The summer I was allowed to get contacts was the same summer my extended and immediate family flew cross-country to Las Vegas for my grandparent's fortieth anniversary. Except, in nearly all the pictures from this trip, I'm wearing glasses. Glasses as round as my face at that age, picking up the sun in every direction. But I can't remember what my mother said or intimated about my not wearing my contacts. Maybe she thought the less often I wore them, the more affordable they could be. Maybe my sister, who also had contacts, was protecting me from afar. However, I had begged for contacts and was now leaving my glasses poolside at the motel while I swam, I was pushing them back onto my nose every time I turned to look out the window. The window of a minivan my mother had rented, despite no one else in my family caring to join in as she drove us to California and the Grand Canyon and Mexico. And now I can't connect the time it would take to even drive us to Mexico from Las Vegas, while the rest of our family sat behind slot machines.

Though, I also imagine these are the lines of parenting. How every part of you slowly achieves a new bandwidth until the vigilance and excitement you hand over to your children is not even noticeable to you, drains and refills, all the way to Mexico. So much so, I realize it's possible that I'm readying to become a single parent simply because I was raised by one.

In fact, mine was a single parent set against two kids, both under ten, months into a mortgage on a new house, surrounded by two acres of yard work, an hour commute, and whatever psychic vestige remained was likely occupied by the grief of widowhood, by the loss of youth. And this was a situation into which she never opted.

If this is what I came from, what currents oversaw me, then surely my want to be a single father to a single child—absent of debt, no lawn to manage, with a flexible work schedule, a clean bill of health excepting the occasional photophobia, and who is signing onto this position with a willingness to spend the rest of his life careworn and in love with someone who is not guaranteed nor responsible for loving him back—surely, to become a single parent in such a design is far more manageable.

And this is exactly the argument I hand over to the world.

When the campaign goes up, Jessie suggests we get together at a brewery on Broad, which none of us venture over to since the downtown location started making pizza. It's the first place I remember going to in Memphis, in a time when I didn't live there yet but visited often: rows of picnic tables in gravel set so close to the train tracks that the locomotion is deafening when it passes, literally takes the sentences from your lips and obliterates them.

Outside, Jessie gathers us beer and we open my laptop, its screen sunstruck so that we tilt it back and forth, Jessie's products a glimmering ribbon at top, arranged like a silent auction. Finally, at an angle we can see, we refresh the page and fifty dollars appears in the tracker, with the name "Anonymous J."

"While I was inside," she says, holding up her phone. I try to say I don't even know how to thank her, but she swats away any words I have to share and reaches past me to hit refresh.

Over the next few hours, some of our shared friends come and go, some of them giving donations, others bringing me a drink instead, which I'm unclear how to interpret. As the sun fades out, the screen becomes more visible, so I constantly adjust the brightness and move it out of view. The last time I look, there's just over two-hundred dollars.

At the end of the night, the amount is stalled at two-forty and we both finish our last sips, Jessie thinking aloud about ways to boost the post, suggesting this collaboration may not be the end of our friendship but its embarkment. What I don't tell her is the amount, though small, is entirely from her sharing it around. I haven't sent it to any family or close friends or liminal friends, and I'm uncertain if I will. More likely, halfway through the campaign, I'll make several anonymous donations, enough to make it seem like a success. From all angles, this is the better approach. Jessie gets the reassurance, the money still comes my way, and the world at large, or the world as it applies to me, will see what the campaign raised and know I'm supported, that there are so many out there who believe I should be a parent, are betting on this reality, when a freight train's light opens onto us. Its sound shells our ears, causing Jessie to turn away and plug the sides of her face; yet, my face stays focused on the leadlight, its intensity overwhelming my vision until it activates a memory, begins to stream it right into my eyes.

I am in the yard of my childhood home, five years old, maybe six, and I am standing on the concrete driveway that separates the front yard from the backyard. The sun overhead is absurdly bright inside this memory, on par with this very moment, something capable of erasure, and my mind is circling a warning from my mother, from relatives, from strangers far and wide, saying you should not stare at the sun. Only, what I hear is: you cannot look at the sun, as in there's a challenge to bad had. That it's the pain that overtakes you that you must avoid. So I choose instead to angle my head upward at the sun and I stand there unblinking, its deadly light invading every pore of my body until it warms my brain. I stay like this for as long as I can. And I do the same the next day. And the next week. And from the backseat of the car. All the way until this vacation in Vegas when my mother has insistently driven us as a family of three to the edge of the Grand Canyon, our feet set atop its cliff, and my head is again pushed straight up at the sun that surrounds us, doing everything it can to not break eye contact, when I hear her voice fall across me.

"Hey," she says. "Look down."

Tethys

People have told me alligators turn up in the bayou now and again. Little ones. Though, little ones that could still grow. Other people have said this has never happened, but there are parrots across the city that have spawned for two decades, ever since an international bird expo was held downtown and the birds did what birds do: flew away. Other people have told me that's not why the birds are in New Orleans, that colonialism does not stop.

The gallery was technically on Julia but too far off from the other galleries to monetize foot traffic. Weeks before reupping the lease, a Rouse's was set to go in around the corner, and a set of offices with a low census was slated for redevelopment into food halls and yet another boutique hotel. All of which would make the location shinier, ripe. But the parking lot to Rouse's was built out of sight of the gallery and the owner of the office building entered a divorce that forestalled the venture.

Mostly the gallery stayed profitable through private buyers. Still, the artist-owner, Michele, wanted it open on track with the others three blocks down: eleven to six, Thursday through Sunday, occasionally later for events, playoff weekends.

This arrangement provided me a corner storefront in which to do whatever I pleased, provided I washed the windows regularly and showed some blanket charm to the few passers-through, all under the minimal supervision of Michele's proxy, Kirstin, who more often than not sent me on errands in her Range Rover to Home Depot or for sushi.

On Thursday, when Kirstin called to say she was going to Houston to visit her brother at MD Anderson, I was intent on watching movies and finishing applications to grad school when Patty walked in, her expression too fucking loony to just let me be.

That morning, I'd been long-winded about the gallery with Jen. She was on her way to UNO, already late, and I hadn't realized I was mounting a rant until it was coming out, my main complaint being that Kirstin's departure put me on duty for White Linen Night.

"Keys?" she asked.

"Kitchen," I said, and continued on. "I'm just saying, if the die-in comes together, I'm going to be stuck inside."

"Why?" she called from the other end of the railroad.

"Cause Kirstin won't be there."

"Just close the doors for a half-hour, say you thought there was a riot, that's how they'll report it anyhow. I have to go," she said, but her body was still paused in the middle of the house.

"I don't know if I can do that," I said.

"Then, I don't know, don't go to the die-in. Where are my sunglasses?"

"That's the whole problem. I need this job, but it's going to look like I'm choosing to be part of the gallery class. It's not like I'm missing the action just for work. No one ever has a problem with that."

"I mean, you already have a job you likely took from someone else. So, quit, I guess," she said and found a different pair of sunglasses than the ones she normally wears in an old bag.

"My job covers rent right now."

"Then we don't make rent," she said, walking out the door.

The gallery's desk space is tucked in the back. It's visible walking in but engagement with the art was Michele's priority. Whenever someone walks in, she explained, I should rise up and move to the other side of the desk, but pretend I'm leashed to it. Show invitation, servility, but never crowd.

When Patty walks in, however, she makes a beeline past the art, her tongue undressed from her mouth in a slew of words I don't fully grab as I close out Netflix on the screen and straighten my jeans.

"I've been sent here by the gods of Harrah's to find something expensive," she says and takes a seat opposite me.

"This is nice," she says, touching the desk, a massive heap of metal collage with a glass surface that is impossible to clean beneath.

"Michele made it," I say.

"She welds?" she asks, and I motion to a lineup of small figure sculptures behind her, all mounted to heavy plinths, their bodies molten and overworked.

"They're beautiful," she says, standing closer. "But I want a painting. Something that eats up a wall. Like that one," she says, pointing behind the desk, where an 8x10 is hung by only two nails so that I must adjust it each time the air conditioning kicks off.

"It's my favorite," I say, which sounds like a queasy thing to say aloud but is, in fact, the truth. It's a piece of canvas Michele dyed and then glazed, the only disruption a sunspot of cadmium yellow center-right.

"It's fifteen-thousand," I say.

"That's a lot," she says, but not in a dismissive manner.

"I might be able to get it down, but it's not my call, I'm afraid."

"Hmm," she says and steps back to take a picture, before texting.

"Are you from New Orleans, born here I mean?" she asks, as she stands tapping at her phone.

"No, Michigan," I say.

"Oh!" she says and clutches her phone between her knees, looking at her palms before deciding the correct one to turn toward me. Using her opposite hand, she pretends to drive her finger around the state. "Where at?"

"Lansing," I say, and she stops her finger like she's arrived at the house I grew up in.

"What about you, Louisiana?"

She shakes her head. "Colorado, Tennessee, Utah. Mostly Tennessee now," and her phone dings.

"Verdict's in," she says. "You find out what you can get me off that one, and we can make a deal tomorrow."

⊙

White Linen Night is a summer block party spread across Julia, its patrons all dressed like they've disembarked the same yacht, a kind of anti-second line for the St. Charles populace. It contains loud music but no rhythm, art on demand but no message.

Two weeks earlier, a young Black girl died in a medical transport out of Gentilly when the ambulance popped a tire during rush hour and was forced to wait seventeen minutes for another vehicle. At the same hour, a white football player was taken by helicopter from Jesuit to Ochsner to treat what turned out to be non-life-threatening dehydration.

The media all covered the story with the same consideration: the girl experienced unpopular side effects to a shot of epinephrine that could not be prevented, though many medical professionals disagreed.

In response, a group of organizers were quietly plotting a die-in to take place on the same Saturday as White Linen Night. They successfully arranged to have the hired DJs stop playing at dusk, while others lay on the ground in silence for seventeen minutes as papier-mâché helicopters attached to helium balloons floated overhead. White allies were to be a kind of guardrail between those presenting the action and anyone looking to disrupt the scene.

Last weekend, Jen and I stood in a warehouse rehearsing in the Marigny, watching the first prototyped medevac lift slowly above us and drive thirty feet up to the ceiling, where the balloons popped on the rusted beams and fell back down to our feet.

"Let me get this straight," Jen says, and she places an onion in front of me to cut, opening a beer. "You get ten percent on anything that's sold while you're in the gallery, even if you don't actually do anything to sell it?"

"Pretty much."

"So, fifteen-hundred dollars just for sitting there."

"Well, not quite. Kirstin said I could negotiate as low as twelve. She said Michele doesn't even like the painting."

"Have you always had a commission rate?"

I shrug yes.

"Ok. So, what's the problem you're having?"

"I think I'm going to make the sale and then quit. It'll cover two months here and grad school apps. It's enough time to find something else, and then I don't have to worry about missing the die-in."

Jen takes a full sip.

"I want to be supportive, but it's weird to find out your job can actually be lucrative, and that you want to quit in the same sentence."

"You get commissions for selling cars, too," I say.

"I guess you do," she says, smiling. "Two months of okra and onions it is," and she dumps my cutting board into a pan.

I do not give a shit about the art on Julia. Not the commercial banquets of color and silhouettes Michele pushes; not the high-concept John Waters' installations down the way; not the kitschy paintings of moonlit sugar cane fields, which eliminate the brutality of harvest. All of these spaces are priced and parceled to serve Uptowners and their houses that look like wedding cakes, their mannered lingua franca of racism, their collective net worth enough to reshoe the coast.

In moving to New Orleans, questions of why spread out from people's lips. Asks on whether or not the oil had been fully cleaned, of how many years before it's underwater, of how to live in a place so segregated. The last always the most frustrating addendum, as if to imply the segregation of any one city was not the segregation of another; as if to suggest separation was something to navigate forever, that humans are an immiscible buildup of atom and emotion.

In college, some of my friends traveling abroad were instructed to iron on Canadian flags, red maple leaf patches to their bags, to mark them as something not American. A safer repute to walk around under. I could never bring together how this worked, if it made it impossible for Americans to be seen as anything less than their worst parts or if it slowly corroded the world's impression of Canada.

When I moved to town, I found a place at the center of Uptown, just off from Audubon Park, an apartment buried in mansions. It was a decision to be a white person who moves to the white part of town, to go where others were quietly prolonging moneyed histories, to camp beside them and smolder, to iron an American flag into the lawn so they could watch me walk overtop it.

Working on Julia was the first of many ways I let all those intentions become blood-let, until passing opinions from neighbors were met with passive looks, until weekends were spent window-shopping houses, imagining gutted double-shotguns with kids growing out of them, lazy stroller walks to the zoo, steering toward a day that flag might become something dusted off and raised enough to catch the wind, because colonialism does not stop.

I walk to the gallery on Friday, a good three-mile route to clear my thoughts, talking to Kirstin as I go. She works to train my inner negotiator, supporting the effort as my sale, not the gallery's, and one I should own and take pride in. She wants me to be operatic about it, show Patty that I want Patty to have this painting, that, for some unchecked reason, I have spent the night imagining Patty and her family eating beneath this painting as it fills a dining room, that I can see Patty's grandkids playing underneath it in their living room, her own kids taking photos of the scene and shoving them into albums they'll revisit in twilights. This painting is not a painting, but a blush of magic to inherit.

I almost say then and there that this will be the last weekend I work, when I remember the only reason Kirstin's in Texas.

"How's your brother?" I ask.

"He's fighting," she says. "The doctors say he's making progress, but—hard to tell."

"You told me he loves a fight," I say.

"He does. He's tough."

When we hang-up, Kirstin has left me with a final piece of instruction: to go into the storage embankment of the gallery's kitchenette and fish out enough pieces of plywood and packing moss to arrange in front of other paintings.

"Make it feel like things are flying off the wall," she says.

However, arriving through the back, I see Patty is waiting out front. The gallery doesn't open for another half hour, but I make a show of opening it all the same and inviting her in, offering coffee. In the back, I have to literally remove the Keurig machine Michele gifted us from its box and get it going, as both Kirstin and I hated the taste. All the while, Patty is determined to comment on everything.

"Did you move down here from Michigan to work with this artist? No!" she says, as if guessing my birthday. "You came here for college."

"Neither," I said. "I had a good visit here once, and that was all it took."

"I love that," she says. "That's impulsive."

Bringing her coffee forward, cup and saucer, she is standing behind the desk beside the painting, looking at its backside. I set the coffee on the opposite side to try and shuttle her away from it, but she picks it up immediately so that we stand like clams in front of the painting.

"It's light," she says.

"Michele and her husband build all the frames. They use pine, but they insert metal dowels, so they stay lightweight and set at the corners," and I pull a smaller painting from the back to show her beneath the canvas.

"So sneaky," she says. "How'd we do on price?"

"So-so," I say. "Michele said we can cover the sales taxes, which knocks about a thousand off."

"Fourteen," she says, and steps back to admire it. I hear Kirstin telling me to paint her a scene, to explain the infinitude of art.

"Here's my dilemma," Patty says. "We obviously didn't drive down here in a cargo van, so to get this up to Montana will cost a bit."

"Montana. Not Tennessee?"

"This guy's going to the lake house," she says. "We have this giant ugly wall that's been open for months. It's driving me crazy whenever we're up there. If you can do fourteen with shipping costs. You have a deal."

"We've never negotiated shipping before," I say. "Let's do it."

"Yeah?"

"I'll pack it up today."

"Wonderful! My husband's going to think we were swindled, but I'll vouch for you," she says, her hand touching a smaller work of plexiglass art catching light in the window. "This is pretty."

"Here," I say, walking over and pulling it off. "As a thank you," and I take the square of color to the table to wrap.

"No, no, I couldn't," she says, but I wave her off, having watched Kirstin make the same gesture time and again.

"My husband wants to stop and see it, if you don't mind waiting a day or two to pack it up. What's the deposit?" she asks, unshouldering her purse.

I look to the table behind me where the credit card reader sits neatly out of sight, only revealed for times of purchase. However, I don't know how to use it.

"No deposit," I say. "We just need a copy of your credit card and license to hold it."

"Even better," she says, handing me her entire wallet.

Saturday morning, Jen drops me at the gallery, my face groggy and worn, having spent the night mostly out. There was another practice for the action, but it was only confirming head counts, with nineteen people set to die and another thirty slated to keep a perimeter. We spent less than an hour in meetup, before ending at several bars outside the quarter.

"Are you recommending a replacement to Kirstin?" Jen asked, holding a burger to her eyes as if using it to measure her mouth.

I shook my head no.

The job was one pulled blindly off Craigslist, a single interview, where I was told there were many others in consideration. When I was given the shot, it seemed like a moment to be proud of, until Jen pointed out that I was twenty days old to New Orleans, that it's unlikely I was competing against other sociology majors for the role, and I could easily have been mistaken for someone who might prevent a theft.

"Maybe she still has a list of the others she interviewed," I said.

Jen nodded, but the rest of the night I realized there was no way.

I decide that will be the effort I make on my final day, to scour Facebook pages and send group texts to try and recruit a batch of better names to pass along, when I find three voicemails blinking away. All hang-ups, minutes apart, from Michele.

On my phone, I have a missed call from Kirstin an hour earlier, along with a text to call her when I make it in.

"So, Michele's not happy," Kirstin says. "It's the free shipping. Apparently, it made her feel commodified."

"But you said I could go as low as twelve," I say. "This is over thirteen after shipping."

"You don't have to tell me. You did everything right in my eyes, this is just a sticking point for her I never thought to mention. I walked into the same trap years ago."

"Ok," I say, sensing there's more in her voice than a hiccup.

"I hate this, I really hate this. Michele wants me to let you go. She thinks it's not the right fit any longer."

I stay silent, realizing there's a gap of relief where there should be self-doubt.

"Do I still get the commission?"

"Do you still—of course! That is your sale. I would never let that be taken from you. I'm going to pad on a couple hundred for severance even. Least that I can do here. This is really, truly my fault for never saying."

"No, it's not a problem," I say, but catch up to the fact that I should not show joy either. "I know if this was your decision, you'd help me improve, and that's why I love working with you."

"Fuck. You're going to make me cry all over again today."

"Don't do that. In fact, I know a few people who might be a good fit, maybe I can leave you a list?"

"God you're gracious. That would be great. And I'm going to come straight in tomorrow to help out. This is all a lot of bullshit you're caught in."

"No, don't worry. You've been traveling all week, I'll clean up," I say.

"Then, lunch! Thursday, lunch on me, we'll go anywhere you want. Jen, too."

When Jen makes it to the gallery, she's dressed in total contrast of the bodied streets, black pants, black turtleneck. This ensemble agreed to in order to help contrast those dying-in, who will be dressed in the same white as the attendees having spent the last several hours ingratiating themselves to the crowd.

She walks in as if gasping for air.

"Christ, it's too hot for these clothes," she says, and hands over a bag of my stuff to change into.

"Fast," she says. "Everyone's already down there."

I had texted Jen everything earlier, but reiterate it all start to finish as I lock up, recess the lights.

"I swear you could fall into a well and not break a bone," she says.

"What?"

"A stranger comes in and basically gives you a thousand dollars, then you decide to quit, and rather than having to go through the awkward part, you're going to get a lobster and extra money."

I pull a long-sleeved shirt over myself.

"I don't really like lobster," I say.

"The point is you're lucky."

At Julia and Camp, everyone is already gathered, spare dots of allies once indistinguishable from the crowd now form a small black hole into which we join, and people around us are just beginning to take notice of this phenomena when the music fades. First one DJ, then another. On their cues, we form a wide ring and begin to fill in with the bodies of the dead, reposed in serried order, so that they look like tally marks on the pavement.

At each turn—those of us fending off patrons—we announce which minute we've entered, making the exhaustive lead up to seventeen all the more paralyzing.

Around us, some shout or try to muscle their way in so they can walk between the bodies, but enough of us are linked together and they don't press farther on. A few of the patrons readily accept what's happening and they stand stilly by, some even removing sunglasses, hats, in respect, even though the sun can barely keep its head above the buildings at this hour.

At minute twelve, when the agitation feels full-blown, several of the black borders move toward the papered helicopters that sit at the center of the bodies. They split open the packaging tape that's held the balloons inside and remove the small weights keeping their landing skids in place. Above us all, yellow balloons come together by the dozen like two displays of sun and slowly lift the helicopters.

At fifteen, the wind coming off the river begins to collide, rocking them about like aerialists in fight. We all watch as the bodies below make it to their feet. They place their hands above their heads one at a time, until they all stand with their arms stretched skyward, their souls handed over.

At seventeen, they form a line and begin to walk away as the rest of us gather anything left over, bags and shoes and headbands, the material that could not transport, and we follow them toward City Hall.

Jen and I stand at the far end of the circle and are the first to begin picking things up. Others follow behind, and my arms are filled with the many garbage bags that had kept the helicopters covered when I look up to find Patty. She is dressed in a white tank top, long flowy pants that flap like bedsheets. Beside her, her husband is in jeans and a white polo. She says nothing to me as we stare into the other, her talkative way subdued. I start past her and her husband as Jen takes my arm and pulls me forward.

In previous years, Kirstin explained they used to go all out for White Linen. They hired performers, hosted open bars, held silent auctions to sponsor GNOF. After several years of investing, no reputational payout made its way back to them. This year, Kirstin wasn't even offering discounts, the gallery kept its normal hours. Falling asleep, it occurred to me there was nothing to clean up, nothing to do, other than googling how to run a credit card.

Waking up, however, I remember Patty's husband had wanted to see the painting in person, that I would have to call and offer to see them, to stand in a hollow room and let whatever was said find echo.

Jen is asleep as I get going, and I steal her keys in lieu of the walk.

After speeches at City Hall, the group disbanded as normal. Kirstin and I were still beat from the night before and made dinner at home, occasionally checking the news but not even a line item covered the action. Though, this was expected; if actual death isn't legitimized, its simulacrum should not be either.

A few friends texted where they had found the helicopters, one of them treed itself only a street away, but the other had floated an odd path and made it all the way to Jackson, an impressive half-mile journey. On my phone, the picture of the second was sitting upright in the neutral ground. I couldn't tell if they'd propped it up or if maybe it landed exactly right. I imagined its descent as a seedling, spinning uncontrollably into earth, where it would slowly expel a fan of roots, which would grow from ghostly to dense to sprawling, something small made immense.

Pulling up to the gallery, I realize I left the wrong set of track lights on all night, so that the space was illuminated but artwork facing onlookers was not. Coming in from the garage, I reverse the lights and unlock the door, in case Patty should appear in off-hours.

Instead, I find a package leaning against the wall of the vestibule that's open to the street. It's covered in newspaper, sloppily, no tape, but I know it immediately by shape. Picking it up, the piece of plexiglass I'd given Patty the day before slides right out, slightly dewed. She must have unwrapped to show her husband and immediately tossed away the brown paper I had tied it off in. It's even clear looking at the folds of paper she had tried to recreate the same envelope I'd created in front of her.

On its surface is a Post-it that reads simply: deal's off. All lowercase, no punctuation.

I wipe the piece with the inside of my tee shirt and replace it in the window, rearranging the two others alongside it so that they pose symmetrically to the outside.

At the desk, I clear the voicemails without listening; I find the few pens for which I can take credit for chewing and toss them out; I clear the browsing history of the computer back to its factory date; I run a paper towel over the keyboard, mouse, display. In the only folder I have out are Patty's photocopies, one of her license and one of her credit card, both pages complete with our initials, stacked like bunk beds. At the time, we'd joked this would stand as a citizen's notarization.

I take the copy of her credit card and press it into the shredder. But I hold the license in my hand, unable to do the same thing. Instead, I cut it out from the page and reread the details: name, date of birth, expiration.

I fold it into my pocket and feel my blood returning.

Phosphorous

For about a month last summer—all of August, in fact—my brother-in-law made claims of going blind. He couldn't drive, couldn't use the microwave, took stairs by hand and foot, like something on four legs. It had been only two months since my sister, Claire, had passed away during childbirth, the baby gone with her, and afterward Simon had become silent and not much else. He wouldn't take my family's calls, left plates of food dropped off by friends to rot on the porch, picked apart by nocturnes. In some ways, the blindness was a relief, that predictable confession of a person needing help but not being able to say so. Abby, our other sister, my now only sister, didn't agree with me. Though I suppose that's the way doctors can be.

"This isn't natural, he needs to talk to someone. You can't keep going over there and giving in," she told me.

"But at least he's reaching out," I said, "And besides, maybe there's some truth to it. I've seen him walk cold into walls, Ab."

"You're only building reliance. This is crazy behavior."

"It's said grief can bring on symptoms no one can understand," I told her, "Medically speaking even, it changes a person."

"Yes, I realize that—" she said.

"Then it's possible. It's possible he's going blind."

By September, shapes began to rematerialize, colors filled back in, Simon's house became slowly cleaner, livable. Over Christmas, he and I took our annual camping trip down to Tennessee; we slept on the overhangs of rock, and we took in the matte of long, silent nights. Nothing above or below but pinpricks of stars that shadowed the ends of nature, making us feel like we had flattened into two dimensions while everything around us bubbled with shape. We drove back north on New Year's Day, and Simon returned to work.

We arrive to this August, and Simon has called me over his house, informing me not to knock, but to meet him around back. I follow his instructions, thinking little, and then there he is: sitting in a piece of patio furniture, a baby cradled asleep at his shoulder. Simon raises a finger, indicating for me to remain quiet, a look on his face like you-have-no-idea-what-it-took-to-get-here.

I sit down across from him. Between us are a half-dozen cardboard boxes: high chair, playpen, some apparatus you bungee between the frame of a door, like he's robbed a Toys "R" Us. Simon smiles at me, softly pouting his lips to make a sound like TV static. He pushes his neck my way, and whispers,

"It's said this sound recreates what was heard in the womb. It calms the child."

I lean forward, and with my palm facing him, fingers fanned apart, I wave my hand in front of his eyes.

"I can see just fine, Marty."

For the next fifteen minutes, we sit. Simon cooing away like a brook, his eyes also closed, and me sitting oppositely wondering about how long I can put off telling Abby. I think of her shaking her head, repeating how I should have listened to her—that this behavior had a future she understood all along. And then the baby wakes.

Simon pats his, or maybe her, back and lifts the child above his eye line, like he's cluing into the biology of foundling thoughts.

"Will you take her a minute? She's probably hungry."

"Simon," I say.

"When I come back out with the formula, I'll explain everything."

He hands her off, and I take her in by the armpits. Simon goes inside, and I raise her up until her eyes meet mine: two, red fruit-fly bulbs that appear incapable of blinking, that seem to be hesitating even more in the sun. I bring her back to my shoulder, and look at the magnolia tree in Simon's backyard. A waxen display of curling petals with a thousand tentacles up and down, all on plates of leaves, like they're serving their bloom. This time of year, it always smells like the after-spray of the perfume counters downtown.

When Claire told me I was going to be an uncle, she could barely get the words out. For three years she and Simon had tried everything, with unwanted and explicit detail. Her ovulation schedule was drawn like a blueprint on poster board, with stick figure diagrams alongside that indicated the positions they'd been making love.

"They say it's partly about variety—because of the entry route,"

Simon told me years earlier, during our first winter excursion into Tennessee, his hand pinched like a duck bill as if to demonstrate "entry route."

"That makes sense," I said, intending to conclude any thoughts of he and my big sister conceiving.

"But Claire doesn't really like all the positions. Is it a family thing, do you have positions you don't like?"

When it finally happened, the two of them had waited until Claire was fifteen weeks to announce anything, so afraid to risk hope.

Simon comes back out of the house, and is shaking sweat off a bottle of formula. He tips the nipple and drops a spot onto his forearm.

"Perfect," he says, and removes the baby from my hold, returning to his patio seat. Like a pro, like he's done it before, he wedges the bottle under lip, and the baby begins to suckle. It's like seeing the universe move.

"Okay. The whole story," he begins.

Simon goes over everything, and in painstaking detail. The trying months, the comedowns in the kitchen, the adjustable mattress they bought to help persuade gravity, all leading up to the afternoon in the delivery room and the moments and images I know too well. Though, slowly, surely, he moves toward an explanation.

"It was after Claire was already pregnant that a friend at St. Luke's approached us about their adoption list," he tells me.

"Since no one cause could be pinpointed for our infertility, we didn't think it wise to invest in treatments. We figured that if the treatments didn't work, we'd have spent the money we could have spent on an adoption in one wash."

"Makes sense," I say

"So when we had the opportunity to get on this list, we thought we better not waste it, pregnant or not. Well. Two years later, and apparently our names kept moving up—I hadn't even thought about getting her name off. God knows I did everything else, canceling her email accounts, the magazine subscriptions, the insurance policies—"

"The cheese of the month club."

"Exactly! That fucking cheese of the month club. But never the list. And then a week ago, they called."

"The hospital called," I say.

"They called, asked if we were still interested. And I said yes."

I look up at Simon, his face as ecstatic as a pinwheel, and I have no idea what to say. I look at him with the same I-have-no-idea-how-we-got-here.

"Amelia," he says to the child, "This is your Uncle Marty."

But Amelia keeps taking down the formula, two inanimate arms straitjacketed in front of her, like broken wands of magic.

Walking into Mercy Health, I don't know which words to elect to tell Abby, but I need to tell someone. I need to compare rationalities with someone I trust. Yet, I'm still nervous to bring anything up, and for fair reason.

There was an evening during the period Simon believed he was blind that I had convinced him to leave the house. We went to a restaurant nearby where Abby and a few others were having dinner, intent on stopping by for a drink, the only goal to return Simon to some normalcy. Regrettably, most of those friends worked with Abby at the hospital, and sitting a not-necessarily-blind blind man into a booth of medical professionals turned out how one would expect. Halfway through, Simon fumbled his way out of the restaurant, knocking over plates and bumping across a tide of patrons clogging the door.

As I went after him, Abby had pulled me aside, furious.

"This is out of control, Marty."

"Look, it won't last forever, but right now we need to support him."

"No. We don't. He's a brother-in-law, Marty, not a brother. Sooner or later, he's going to have to move on and make his own life. Maybe this is that point."

I didn't reply to her then, and she never apologized after, leaving it to be a truth we hadn't untethered.

Abby comes into the waiting room with her hair half out of its ponytail, a few blots of something still damp on her pant leg, and a sweatshirt zipped over her scrubs.

"I have ten minutes," she says, "And do not ask what's on my leg—anything would be a guess today."

We're outside on the hospital's campus and walking for a coffee cart when it occurs to me the longer I wait to tell her, the less time we'll have to discuss, but I can't push the sentences together any faster.

"What is it you wanted? Linda said you looked flushed when you asked to see me."

"It's Simon, actually."

"Oh god, don't tell me he has you worried about me, too."

"Worried about you?" I ask.

"He calls me last night—middle of the fucking night, no idea why he's even awake—I see it's him, I pick up in a panic, and all he wanted to talk about was my love life. He thinks I'm putting too much into my job, that I deserve a family."

"He said the word family, not just boyfriend or husband?"

"A whole family. And the worst part is, I don't disagree. I'm thirty-three, I do want a family, but I haven't been putting it off, either. It simply hasn't been."

"No, of course not. We know that. I'm sure he knows that, too."

"So you're not here about that?"

"No," I say, and I turn toward her. "I really just stopped by to see you."

When Claire left for college, I carried all my stuff into her room, but didn't fix it up any. It was my senior year, and all I really wanted was the extra space and privacy it provided. The walls remained a dull rose, her dresser still like a perfume counter: the heads of many glass vials in series, with knit atomizers attached like the bellies of spiders.

On the ceiling of her room, years before, she had glued up two bags of plastic glow-in-the-dark stars: Pegasus, Hydra, Andromeda, Lepus. The constellations blushed an alien green beneath her door at night, and I used to keep mine open just to see the color bleed out, like she'd yanked down the Northern Lights and was holding them hostage in her closet. I could recall looking up at them the day I moved in, how all their light was emptied, something without purpose just cobwebbed to the ceiling.

Walking into Simon's house the following day, I find him in Amelia's nursery pressing up those same kind of fake glow-in-the-dark stars with a broom handle, and I can hardly breathe.

"Do you remember these things?" he asks, and I nod.

"Claire used to talk about them all the time, how one day we'd put them up on our kids' ceilings. I didn't remember, of course.

I'm shit with things like that, but this morning when I was loading up Amelia's dresser, I found three packages of them in the bottom drawer. She bought them without ever saying."

I look around the nursery, which I'm now realizing has never been touched. The crib, the rocking chair, the appropriate books and stuffed menageries are all as they had been a month before my sister's due date. Even the daffodil color Simon and I had painted on at Claire's request still smells freshly contained.

"You never took this room apart," I say.

"I pretty much shut the door the day you dropped me off from the hospital."

I nod, and realize I can't remember the days following Claire's death—or my exact movements, as if someone else entirely had been animating me during that time, just hand-drawn transitions in newsprint that immediately yellowed in my memory.

"Amelia's sleeping?"

"Yeah, in my room," and Simon rotates his hip and taps the baby monitor he has clipped to his belt.

"Actually, I need to talk to you," he says, and rests on his broom limb, clearly chewing through his next words.

"The day I picked Amelia up from the hospital I met her parents—or grandparents, they'd be. I didn't meet her mother or father, just the mother's parents. They were really thoughtful people, come to think of it, but they were relieved Amelia was going to a nice couple."

"You mean not a widowed single-father?" I ask.

"It didn't really seem the moment to bring it up," he says, "And so I didn't. The grandparents left. I signed the forms, and said Claire would mail hers later."

"You told them that?"

"I just figured I could table the issue, you know? I'd get home with Amelia, grow settled, and then say there must have been some kind of misunderstanding. I assumed I'd just have to pass a character test or something."

"What'd they say?"

"This is where I might need help. I signed Claire's signature and turned in the papers."

"Please say you're kidding."

"The day after I brought her home. I just panicked. I didn't want anyone changing their mind on me, like donor's remorse."

"There's a death certificate, Simon."

"I know that. You know I know that. But that first day: Marty. I lived outside myself. That's not an easy feeling to come across in the world."

"Simon, you have to talk to someone. You need a lawyer, probably."

"I am a lawyer."

"You're not a criminal lawyer."

"They're going to take her away from me, Marty," he says with such defeated intelligence that I know he'd fall over if he let go of the broom.

"I'm beginning to think they should," I say, and right on cue, Amelia's voice breaks through the pinholes of the monitor and drowns us both out.

Two days later, Simon calls and invites me over for dinner. Through the phone, I hear the chirping sounds of Amelia, and I imagine he has the receiver shouldered against his ear as he holds her. I feel restless not to go, but I tell him I have plans. I say maybe I'll be over after, and decide that will be enough. I hear Abby's logic fit between my ears, about how there comes a point.

Claire and Simon had been trying to conceive for eight months when my sister finally broke down in front of us. It was the weekend after Thanksgiving, and we had all gathered at Abby's new apartment. The first place she had on her own since residency ended, but she'd yet to buy any furniture or housewares. We sat on hardwood floor beside a gas fireplace, a crowd of paper plates and pizza boxes, and at the center of us was Claire.

"It just might not happen, and I have to accept that. I might not be a woman who knows what it is to have a child."

"You can still be a mother," Abby said.

"A mother, sure. But all those conversations about the pain, the labor stories, the look on my face. I'll never have that."

"That's minutes on a day," I told her.

Simon put his arm around Claire, and she near-to broke it at the elbow as she threw it off.

"I don't want to be coddled any fucking longer," she said, and left the room. Simon, who I'd never seen behave desperately before, turned to Abby, and Abby went for Claire.

As Simon and I cleared up the living room floor, stacking plates into boxes and searching the cupboards for a garbage bag—which Abby had also yet to pick up—he relented.

"I need to get out of here. I need to get away," he'd said.

"I can drive Claire home, if you want."

"No, farther away. I need a trip. No Claire, no pregnancy, no people. Would you do that with me?"

"You want me to go on your trip of no people?"

"Over the winter, when we both have time. We'll drive some-where, camp maybe. Claire and I aren't doing each other any good right now. We need to breathe," he'd said.

A month later, we drove out of the mounds of snow that had settled, watching the lumps get smaller and smaller as we made it south. Originally, Simon had found a place in Kentucky, but as we made it to the exit, he just kept driving, and I didn't stop him. Something inward had propelled him farther into Tennessee, and we watched together as the mountains emerged from the fog like blue teeth.

It's late when I finally get to Simon's, but he isn't alone. Abby's car is parked on the street, and she's walking to it as I pull up. I can feel my heart slide neatly out of place. I realize I didn't tell Abby when I had the chance, she didn't have time to intervene, and now it's all going to boil over—but she's smiling; she's normal, a blue grocery bag in her hands.

"What are you doing here?" she asks.

"Just stopping around to say hey. Why are you here?"

"Simon asked if I wanted a free meal," she says, holding up the pouch of tin foil.

"You didn't go inside?" I ask.

"Just for a minute. Did you know Simon's babysitting for a co-worker? He has a crib up in the old nursery and everything."

"He told you he was babysitting?"

"You think it's weird, too? What kind of parents leave their new-born with a co-worker?"

I shrug, careful not to be forced into a longer lie, and watch as Abby drives away, two eyes of warning staring back in her wake. I walk slowly for the house, whose lights are all off save for the bedroom. I make it as far as the door, but I don't knock. Instead I linger at the front window, where I can see the otherworldly starlight of Amelia's room at blur behind the curtains.

When we were younger, and Claire served as live-in babysitter, she would create elaborate blanket forts through our split-level. Abby and I would wait on the couch in awe as she worked, using chairs to stilt up the angles, and picture frames to hold them secure, some kind of high school architect who knew everything we didn't. She would finish, walk Abby to one opening and me to the other, and race us like we were lab equipment. We'd finish a half hour later maneuvering the booby trap coat hangers that could collapse a tentpole if we didn't move slowly enough, while our big sister sat on the kitchen counter with a bowl of ice cream melting in her lap. I imagine Claire wouldn't have let Simon put up those stars so quickly, that she would have wanted to wait until Amelia could understand what she was looking at, about arrangement, about the language of maps. I imagine there are a lot of things Claire would never do.

I get back in my car, and call Abby. I tell her we need to talk.

Simon's parents passed away several years before, his father after college, his mother after he finished law school. He has two siblings, both brothers who live on the West Coast: one a dentist, the other flips houses. Though, for the better part of a decade, he's been with my family. Come Thanksgiving, Christmas, Easter, that amalgam of holidays that seem religious even when they're not.

The upshot is my parents have taken to him like another son. Even still, as I pull into Simon's driveway after work on Friday, their car being out front, if not a surprise to Simon, is a devastating one to me.

The night before, Abby was impossible to calm down over the phone. She seemed to blame me for protecting Simon, for endangering a child, and despite her being the younger voice of reason, I knew she was right. I had overlooked too much, and now that misstep had led to our parents—the two of them probably inside whisking Amelia through the air as they flap their lips like a helicopter.

I enter in through the garage, which leads to the kitchen, and there's my mom: a burp cloth over one shoulder, Amelia's two beady eyes now full open and receiving all those atoms of memory she'll too-soon forget.

Through the window above the sink, I can see my father and Simon standing in front of the magnolia out back, both with beers in their hands, feet kicking aloft its fallen petals

"There's Uncle Marty," my mom says, "Or is it uncle-in-law? Is there such a thing?"

"I wouldn't begin to know what my relation is," I say.

"Well, Amelia seems comfortable around us," she says as she guides her body toward me, and my mother kisses my cheek.

"You didn't tell me Simon's brother was in town with this one. He said he's been babysitting all week."

"His brother?" I ask.

"His brother, Ben. Simon said you've been over twice already."

I look out the window where both men's backs are still turned away from me.

"Where's Ben now?" I ask.

"Store, business meeting, I don't know," she says, applauding Amelia's nose with her own.

"So you two were just stopping by?"

"No, Simon invited us over, for the cookout. Didn't he mention it to you?"

"What cookout?"

"He called the whole family for a little summer get-together. That reminds me, Abby said she couldn't make it till late. I think she's stressed again. Have you two talked?"

I look back at my mother, whose hairstyle hasn't changed in three decades, the same halo of curls she has dyed every month, two gold earrings, which hug the lobes. The day Claire's water broke, my mother had dressed in dark burgundy pants.

"Polyester," she said, pinching the fabric in the waiting room.

"They're nice," I told her.

"You can clean them easy."

"Has that been a problem lately?" I asked.

"Deliveries are a dirty business, my boy," she said.

I look at the way she clings to this false grandchild now, and I can see the same excitement she found that day in the smallest of changes. How she'd expected those changes to prolong, for grand-children to love her endlessly, to update her. There comes a point, I think.

"I forgot something at the office," I say. "I need to make a quick run."

"Okay, sweetie. Though you're not getting through that door without a kiss," she says, and angles Amelia's cheek in my direction until it presses against my lips, and for the briefest moment I feel thankful we never remember what it is to be small.

In the driveway, however, I find my car blocked in. Behind it is a car I don't recognize and, along the street, come two more cars slowing to park in tandem: my Uncle Kenny and Aunt Rita in their pickup, and our cousin Wendy with her two little ones in the sedan. I move across the yard to get a better look at exactly who's in the car behind mine, and just as I do a police cruiser pulls half into the drive, taking one tire onto the curb—everything at once working upon a collapse. I know instantly Abby wasn't willing to wait on me, and even more that she wasn't able to do something on her own, either. A woman gets out of the car, greets the police officer, and both move up the drive in my direction. From the backdoor of her car, unlashing the car seats, Wendy turns and raises her arms up in the air as if I might be able to pantomime to her exactly what's happening.

"Simon Busa?" the woman asks me.

"I'm sorry," I say.

"Are you Simon Busa?" she repeats.

"I am," Simon says from behind me, and I turn to find him standing at the edge of the garage door, my mother and father alongside. He puts his beer down on the concrete and takes Amelia from my mother's arms.

"Okay," he says to her. "We're okay."

After the light in the plastic stars ran out, I found Claire standing on her bed, holding a flashlight against each one, and counting to thirty. She moved end to end, like some keeper of stars who had fallen out of the universe, and was trying to maintain her purpose. One after the next, to thirty, to thirty, until she pulled her curtains shut, closed the door, and we both looked up together wondering where the glow could have gone.

Simon doesn't come around for Thanksgiving or Christmas. On both occasions, either Abby is short with me, or I'm short with her. In any case, she and I speak little. The story of him taking in Amelia, of forging our dead relative's signature, of pretending to be an entire family circulates through both dinners. It invades everything, everyone with a different opinion on the matter, those there recounting the scene of Simon insistently trying to get to Amelia's diaper bag before the officer finally restrained him to the backseat. They repeat the way Simon couldn't even look at anyone, how he just lied down in the cruiser, as if it wasn't too late to hide. "Honestly, you don't rob a bank and invite everyone to the spending spree," Uncle Kenny says each time. It's too inopportune a moment to defend a person, over those holidays. Doing so is like catching wind in a jar: just because you've done it, it doesn't mean it'll still blow your hair when you open it later.

I had followed Simon to the police station that day, where he was held for questioning, but he was released until the issue could be fully evaluated. Psychological tests were to be administered, followed by contacting the girl's mother. The social worker and police officer, however, had not seemed as angered as my family. Both even offered to return to the house and inspect where Amelia had been staying should the need to testify on his parental fitness arise. They wanted to trust him the way we hadn't. Though, after I dropped Simon off back at home, he stopped taking my calls, stopped coming to the door.

For most of that time, it occurs to me it might not have been about us reaching an end with Simon, but rather his reaching an end with us. I think about how badly he wanted to be a father, about what it took for him to finally have that moment. I think of what it would be if on the same day both the person I loved most and the impossibly fragile thing we'd grown to life were taken away. I try to think about what I'd cling to, about what I would no longer want to see.

The morning after Christmas Day, though, Simon knocks on my door, and I answer to find him outside with his truck. In its bed, I see our usual tents and coolers and kerosene lamps tied in place, as he stands at my front step with falling snow piling into his hair. He looks at me the way he had in years past, a person with no people, and I reach for my jacket.

Antimatter

I read somewhere that if we were to catch all the lightning—the four-million-some land strikes that occur each and every day, bar none—if we caught all that lightning for one year, we'd be able to run the Earth uninterrupted for nine full days before the lights started to flicker. It can be calculated down to the minute, those nine days, like turning over a large hourglass. I read somewhere else, however, that the temperature of a lightning bolt is, on average, 50,000 degrees Fahrenheit. The surface temperature of the sun is only 10,000 degrees. So even if we imagine storing that much kinetic energy in one central unit, the consequences of overheating are equivalent to putting a tank of helium in a microwave. Still, that's not exactly the kind of messaging you want to share when going door-to-door.

At the first Ecolytes meeting I ever attended, I was given a two-inch pack of reading, which included everything from paraphrased governmental research to telemarketing scripts, lapel stickers that read: "Nuclear Today, Gone Tomorrow," even a notecard disclaimer explaining all materials had been printed on paper created from organic plant material; the pages felt furred and sodden when held for too long.

I was suckered into donating to the group outside a Walgreens, where a Planned Parenthood foot soldier had cornered me on my way.

"Excuse me," she said. "Can I ask how your day is going?"

"Fine," I said. "But I already give monthly."

"To Ecolytes?"

"Oh," I said. "I thought you were out here for Planned Parenthood," pointing to her shirt where the group's insignia blazoned her chest, two consonants huddled together against a storm.

"An easy mistake. However, Ecolytes is an organization that doesn't believe in investing resources where they can be avoided."

"What do you invest in?"

"Environmental reparations. Our work engages awareness around the economic impacts of the climate crisis, and how to reconcile existing consequences. Don't get me wrong, we're all for preventative measures, but we don't have the greatest faith in the powers that be."

"I'm sorry, I've never heard of you."

"We're relatively new. Here," she said, passing along a flyer on which billows of blast furnace-smoke formed the letters of their name. "Any questions you have can be answered at one of our info sessions. I'm Tania."

"Kori."

"Well, I hope to see you again. Oh, Kori—while I have you, you're not going in there to buy tampons, are you?"

"No, just milk."

"Right on. See you soon."

The next time I saw Tania, she was hugging me as if she'd sent me off in a life raft. Her hair was pulled back in a single plait, and tucked up beneath a purple baseball cap.

"Kori, right?" she asked. "I was just telling someone about you. Come this way."

Six weeks later, I am deemed too valuable for stationary work. I become tasked with going house to house in privileged neighborhoods around Memphis with a partner named Patrice, a mouse-voiced girl a few years younger on mental leave of absence from Vanderbilt, and serving an AmeriCorps term to pass time.

The two of us are sent weekly walking routes at the start of each week by the office manager, who signs his emails with a rotating quote from an environmentally-conscious celebrity: Ed Asner, Whoopi Goldberg, Ralph Nader; the list goes on and on.

Sunday afternoons, Patrice texts to confirm a meeting time, and we appear at the given route bright and early Monday morning, emailing the office manager as a safety protocol, each automated reply returning us a compelling quote we're to share with residents along our way:

"Did you know Michael Douglas called the manmade phenomena destroying our planet more 'mentally unwinding than throat cancer'?" Patrice tees me up.

"With donations like yours, we can improve the lives of those we're affecting—today."

For two months we come together under the same design, the spiels slowly as instinctual as tying shoelaces, the returns on our time invested rarely more than a terminal commitment of twenty dollars. At one house, a woman still on her phone handed us a hundred-dollar bill, and when we explained we couldn't accept cash for security reasons, she'd absentmindedly written a check for a thousand. It cleared an electronic deposit, and we never went back. Beyond that, the collections pay our living wage.

"Sometimes I feel like overeducated beggars," I tell Patrice.

"You might be, but until I start school again, I'm living a very honest reality."

"But you live at home," I say.

"Yeah, but I pay my cell phone, car insurance—I'm hardly off the hook for things."

"Do you think you'll go back in the fall?" I ask.

"I don't know. I think. Did I even tell you why I left?"

"Tania told me it was Chronic Fatigue Syndrome."

"What's that?"

"It's when you have diminished energy and can't rest normally. I googled it before we met," I admit.

"That's not why I left."

"No?"

"Short version: there was an incident with a guy, where I couldn't exactly remember all the details. I was drunk, he was drunk. After that night, I would have panic attacks whenever I saw him. Eventually, I decided to leave and come back when we'd be in different years."

"I'm sorry," I say. "I really didn't know."

"It's fine. For all we know, it wasn't his fault."

"Did you ever ask him about it?"

"No. I was going to. Every time I saw him—I don't know. It just didn't work to ask."

Though it doesn't feel like the right time to approach it, I wonder if Tania knows the real reason Patrice left. Or, maybe I wonder whether or not there was a truth Tania had intuited from me the day we met, something she'd breathed in from a distance, a colorless feature I emitted.

"Anyway. Has anything like that happened to you?" Patrice asks.

By March, Patrice and I have settled into a much closer friendship than originally anticipated, one that transitioned quickly from delivered acquaintance to someone trustworthy, familiar. We go from meeting to carpooling, from seeing each other on weekdays to occasional weekend ventures, including a trip to Arkansas at her aunt and uncle's lake house. No electricity, just two-person games, and sharp blue water that looked like eye color.

We now attend and actively recruit people to info sessions, using the same inflections as Tania, wrapping twine around the intro packets. The office manager has gone from enigmatic avatar to Dean, a thirty-something IT specialist who tells us about the algorithm he's created to populate the quotes we compliment him for sharing.

One week, Tania even asks us to fill in for her, to lead an intro meeting:

"You're ready," she says. "Just remember: your job isn't to convince someone that they've done something wrong. It's to find the people who already care."

"I know," I say.

"You're ready," she repeats.

For my birthday, Patrice buys me a t-shirt that reads: "Every action has a reaction," with a cartoon of a man tossing an apple core in a trash can in one panel, and a tree growing outward from the trash can in the next. Most days, I keep this shirt rewashed as a kind of Muirian ensemble. While I still feel no control over my future, or the bleary stage of life I'm occupying—to act recusant, to feel fight and ignition—it makes life feel less windblown.

It's a Wednesday afternoon when we find ourselves standing outside a manse-sized colonial in Central Gardens, talking to a retired couple, who couldn't be less engaged with our mission. Yet, the sight of two young girls, the age of their own daughters we learn, has created a beeline to their hearts.

"What charity did you say you're with again?" the man asks.

"Not charity," I say. "We're with an organization looking to raise awareness around people who have been unfairly affected by climate change."

The woman looks upward as if to silently call upon the cloudless blue of the sky to object with our existence.

"This must be a tough job for two cute things," she says. "What do you think, Arch?"

"Bonnie Raitt said," Patrice interrupts, glancing at her phone, "'We must be the change we want in the world,' and we believe that means putting others first."

"Bonnie Raitt said that?" the man questions.

"She did," I say, my hand at Patrice's shirt to steer her away from double-checking her phone and revealing the quote from Gandhi—a likely environmentalist but not one of our core sponsors.

By the time the couple closes the door, we've nailed down a two-year commitment of thirty dollars a month, affectionately known as the Matt Damon donor-level, and a first for our local chapter of Ecolytes.

I look to Patrice who is scrolling back to her email.

"Shit me," she says. "Dean's whole system must be fucked. Yesterday, we also told people that Susan Sarandon said: 'Life is not measured by the number of breaths you take, but by the moments that take your breath away.'"

"He must have linked the wrong page," I say.

"Well, I'm calling him," she says, and we step off their walkway, squeezed between the poplar trees of the couple's front yard. In this part of the city everything possesses a thymy, aristocratic scent. Planes cross to and fro, but with enough distance that they go unheard, like crucifixes circling overhead.

Across the street, a black Volkswagen sedan takes a sharp turn up the curb and into a driveway, where a guy with a gym tote crisscrossed over his shoulders pops out. Two fluorescent-colored socks shoved into open-toe Adidas, he keys in his garage code and goes inside. An instant lost cause, I think. But, behind me, Patrice has concealed herself inside the arms of a magnolia, and is bunched over root, her legs buckled, and arms tucked underneath.

"Did you get a hold of Dean?" I ask.

"That's him," she says.

"Who's him?" I ask.

"Justin. He's the reason I left."

By the time we trace our way from Justin's street, and back to where we've parked, Patrice has a smoother line of breathing. In the car, she sits in the passenger seat, bent over her knees with her head pushed to the glove box.

"Did you know he lived in Memphis?" I ask, and she shakes her head unclearly.

"I mean I kinda forgot, but I did know," she says. "Yes."

"We can—"

"I thought they'd stopped," she says.

"The attacks?" I ask.

"I thought they were gone. I've even been looking at pictures of him on Instagram. Like practice, you know?"

"It didn't give you trouble?"

"At first, a little. But, no—it wasn't trouble. I had worked my way there. Writing his name over and over, saying his name aloud, then pictures."

"Did someone suggest that?"

"The counselor I saw. It's supposed to help defamiliarize the experience, like relearning the person on your terms."

I take my hand and rub it across Patrice's shoulders, but the contact feels blank, phantom-like, and I pull away. Instead, I start the car.

"Come on," I say. "I'll take you home."

"No," Patrice sits up, her hair swept across her forehead and balanced there by air-conditioned sweat. She lunges over and swipes out the keys.

"What if you talked to him," she says, all inflection of this ask and the weight it holds removed.

"What?" I say.

"This is happening because I don't know what happened. I can't ask, but maybe you can find out."

"How would I do that?"

"You'd start with Ecolytes nonsense, and then go from there," she says.

"I'm supposed to just come out and ask him about you? When,

after I tell him how increased acid rain is permanently damaging the world's soil chemistry?"

"No, he's on spring break. Ask where he goes to school, say you know me."

"He's not going to come out and say what happened, even if he remembers."

"Kori. If I can't be a hundred feet away, I might as well not go back."

The front door to the Brower's family home is a russet-brown, with a dozen glass panels cut prismatically to blur the images of life inside. After I ring the doorbell, I see him walking toward me from the back of the house, his image kaleidoscopic through the panes, so that dozens of him move toward me unstopping.

Justin smiles immediately, and I force out one to match, his hands holding half a sandwich that is coming apart at the lettuce.

"Hi. My name's Kori, and I'm with an environmental justice organization seeking to create a fund that will provide reparations to those who have been unintended victims of climate change."

"Wow," he says. "I thought this was going to be magazines. Please, keep going."

"We're out here looking for people interested in offering support. This could mean a donation, but more importantly we're trying to have an honest discussion around what many across the world face as a result of manmade pollution. Do you have time to talk?"

"Sure, I have some time."

"Great. Are you home for spring break?"

"I am. Do you go to Vandy?"

"No, I'm not in school anymore. I know a lot of people who do, though."

"Oh, cool."

"Basically, there are a handful of facts and figures we feel best represent the case we're trying to make to people who aren't exposed to the everyday destruction."

"Look, I don't want to be rude, and I have time to listen, but I'm starving. I just got back from a workout. Is it cool if you come inside while I finish making food? Do you want some water, or a sandwich, or something?"

Patrice and I discussed several scenarios for how the conversation might go: Justin shuts the door, Justin hits on me, Justin isn't actually Justin; but none of them included being invited in, which has never been offered on previous routes. Despite what I know, he is unassuming, clear-eyed, with hairless features that age him in reverse. Even still, on the suggestion alone, I feel the tide run out beneath my feet.

"Water would be great," I say.

The inside of the Brower house seems put together in an intelligent manner, with each room having some access to throws and pillows, so that the highborn decor all feels softly touched. Family photographs are arranged expertly out of order on the walls, inlaying the bookshelves: the Brower family at the beach, the Brower family at the Golden Gate Bridge, the Brower family beneath the concatenations of the Eiffel Tower. Ferns, ivy, begonias, all lap the main hall, so that there's an extra amount of oxygen I can almost feel lighten my chest as I follow Justin toward the back of the house.

The kitchen is a bit more predictable, firm wood cabinets and stainless-steel appliances. On the marble island, Justin is piecing together a large sandwich that takes up two cutting boards, olive oil spilling onto the countertop. From the fridge, he grabs a water and places it across from me, at one of the island's stools.

"You sure you're not hungry?" he asks, rinsing off his bread knife.

"I'm sure," I say.

Then: "Thank you," uncertain of how to negotiate the line between polite and skeptical, spy and intruder.

Justin places his dishes in the sink and comes around to the seat beside mine, opening the chair to face me. He's at first too close, but senses this, and proceeds to back up so that we share the bar ledge equally.

"I like your shirt," he says.

I look down, having already forgotten my elected uniform.

"Thanks," I say.

"Okay. You talk, I'll listen," he reasons, and takes a large bite of sandwich.

"Actually, it's better if it's a discussion. That way I can make some notes and get a sense of how people usually talk about climate change."

"Well—," he begins, but a piece of sandwich catches wrong, and he holds his hand up a second to let it pass. Only, it seems to just stick harder the more he raps at his chest. I uncap my water and offer it to him, which Justin attempts to drink, before letting the dribbles slide down the front of his face. Instantly, calm leaves him. He reaches out in my direction, and grabs my forearm, his nails indenting my skin, he leans the weight of his body onto mine like an animal trying to escape a bag. I aim his body toward the counter and, with an open hand, begin to strike between his shoulders, some alarmed motion to jar his body forward. It feels helpless, but I continue, over and over, thinking of the other things to try, until a final whack frees Justin's throat and he vomits onto the island.

A piece of romaine resurfaced on the counter having clogged his windpipe, likely operating as a valve against his throat. He turns to me, the blood vessels of his eyes clipped, his whole face a deeply blood-rushed color of fear.

"Thank you," he mouths, and then ungracefully collapses into the kitchen floor: knees, shoulders, head, unconscious.

I kneel down at Justin's head, his chin still smeared with puke, and I use a paper towel to wipe it off. Why this would be the first instinct, I can't say, but first I wipe his face clean, and then I check to see if he's breathing. My fingers push shakily against his artery. For a minute, I can't quite distinguish between the pulse that exits my fingertips and his life, but slowly, surely, I'm confident he's breathing. Likely, he lost oxygen and fainted. This answer seems simple enough, and so I go with it.

Standing up, I survey the room, almost in a way that suggests I'm looking for clues, trying to unearth a reason for what's happened when I've witnessed the entire alphabet of what went wrong.

My phone is still in the car, and I don't see a landline. On the kitchen table, Justin's gym bag is tossed to the middle, the drawstrings spread open to reveal a scrunched, yelling mouth. Reaching in, I pull out his wallet, keys, and find his phone. I press the home button, but it asks for a passcode. I open his wallet, a goofy license picture of Justin with hair dyed blonde by the sun, his cheeks a full bloom of rosacea. In the wedge is sixty dollars in cash, three twenties folded into fourths, the origami of parents who are always slipping money to their children. Nothing helpful.

In this lull, it's strangely peaceful. Though a small odor is beginning to develop an identity from the island. I wet some paper towels and clear off the counter, tossing them out in the garbage under the kitchen sink. The whole time I do, I'm reiterating those TV movies of people who clean up a crime spree in a panic, and later have to sit in a small room where someone asks: "Well, what made you touch the blood? Why wouldn't you call someone first?"

However, it's only after everything is cleaned that I finally go for Patrice.

Patrice is standing behind Justin's head in the kitchen, clenched with shock. She leans down and places her hand at his head and adjusts his hair, doing so more intimately than emergently.

"Jesus, did you push him?" she asks.

"No, I told you, he passed out."

"Just, passed out?"

"He was choking. It probably cut off too much blood."

Patrice stands and looks around the kitchen.

"Were you two having lunch?" she asks.

I snap my fingers, clap hands; I say his name again, which is like calling after a bird, and his ears twitch, some auditory reflex, but nothing else. Patrice is disinterested in this tactic.

"He's still breathing. Maybe we call someone?" I ask.

"Who, his RA?"

"I'm serious. What if he has a concussion? Do you know anyone from school he might know well?"

"I think we need to leave it be. As long as he's breathing, it's like a bad fall. He'll wake up, he won't remember everything that happened."

Patrice looks around the kitchen, the counter, the table. She picks up Justin's wallet and shakes her head looking at the picture.

"There's money in here," she says.

"I think we should get him off the floor," and Patrice shrugs, tossing Justin's belongings back onto the table and taking his armpits under her hands. Her approach to a lifeless Justin appearing more manageable than compared to a Justin at a distance alive and well.

His body lifts easily between the two of us, and we fold him together to navigate the main hallway, originally thinking we'd get him as far as his bedroom before realizing they're all upstairs.

"The couch," I say, and we steer him onto the armrest, sliding him fully across by his ankles, adjusting his clothes as the friction of the couch teases down his shorts. From the kitchen, I grab several icepacks and wrap them in paper towels, tucking the ice at the back of his neck. Patrice meanwhile seems delirious by where she is, putting a hand over every cornice of his house, peering into smaller cabinets, eyes redoubled, as if her interactions hold some alternate timeline of a relationship that never was.

I can remember back to our trip in Arkansas, where Patrice and I lay on the stilted deck of her aunt's home. It was still too cold to sunbathe any, but the heat felt so real that we lay recumbent on the deckchairs bundled up in thick sweaters with spiked iced teas. It was the only other time Patrice had brought up the incident.

"I think it was hard to see him so often, because I wanted more," she said.

"You wanted a relationship?" I asked.

"Not just a relationship. An entire life. Do you think it's possible to feel that way? Sometimes I think what if nothing wrong actually happened, what if it was just this vacuum effect of missing out on an entire life with someone who didn't want the same thing."

I didn't respond when she said it, but could never dislodge the idea, either. Her ability to still show affection for Justin, as if those months with a counselor, of writing his name over and over in notebooks, had somehow reverted from therapy to consolation to a renewed possibility.

"We should get going," I say, but when I turn around Patrice isn't even in the room.

Upstairs are four rooms. At the top is an office of sorts, with stacks of plastic bins, and a yoga mat unfurled in the middle; across from this quasi-office is a primary bedroom, with symmetrical night-stands and large bay windows, jutting out into the tree line; the remaining bedrooms anchor the corners, separated by a wall made entirely of bookshelves, running floor to ceiling. Inset at the center is a large aquarium, a muted orange light affixed above to heat the water. I tap on its side and watch the fish scatter back and forth.

Approaching Justin's house, I'd actually contemplated taking a long walk around the block instead—never going through with it at all. I saw myself returning to the car a half hour later, back to Patrice, lying right to her face:

"He said you never slept together," I say, playing surgeon to her memory, as if this one night of missed judgment is an obvious, ecto-pic growth.

"How'd you get him to tell you?" she wants to know, her voice barely audible so overtaken with relief.

"I asked how well he knew you, and it just came up," I say, remov-ing the growth, and tossing it outside of her.

"Maybe I was wrong about him, after all," she says, staring into the distance, and like every surgeon, I'd have to realize that I'm removing matter, not personality.

To my right, I find Patrice sprawled faceup on Justin's bed, staring at the ceiling.

"Patrice," I say, but she doesn't pay attention.

"Patrice," I repeat, entering in.

"Just give me five minutes, Kori."

It's unclear just by looking what kind of person Justin is, or into which category he could fall. Nothing in his room gives the impression he would be dressed head to toe in Under Armour, or that the textbooks at his desk would suggest a theology major. By the window is an old computer monitor that's gone to disuse, a duffel of clothes beside it, all of which are folded neatly and packed in place; opposite the bed is a waist-high dresser with a lanyard and meal card, spare change spread across like jewelry. The room does little more than to provide Justin an age.

In the closet are old gameboards, a hamper, the stacks of miscellany youth bring. I remember four birthdays in a row my great-grandmother buying me the same waterproof camera, each year saying, "To use at the beach," which my family hadn't ventured to in a dozen summers. Those items are exactly what Justin has, too: a reliquary of trinkets you don't understand how to part with, so you scatter them to a corner of unreality.

I take a seat beside Patrice, my weight causing the mattress springs to strain and flirt with noise.

"You're not worried about him waking up?" I ask.

"I thought there would be something else up here," she says, and I look around again.

"What else?"

"I don't know," she says.

"You really can't remember anything from that night?" I ask.

She shakes her head.

For a moment, I realize this is exactly what will become of Patrice and me. Our friendship will find dissolution the day she returns to school, the memory of me only resurfacing on winter days when it's inexplicably hot in the world, or some recruitment flyer surfaces outside a dining hall. This day will become a vague experience and all its intimacy weightless.

Patrice's phone begins to buzz, and I flip it over to see who's calling.

"It's Dean. Want me to answer?" I ask.

"Maybe I do have chronic fatigue syndrome," she says.

Downstairs, Patrice waits by the front door, while I check on Justin. The icepacks have warmed and a puddle ekes across the couch pillows. More color has returned to Justin's face and his chest lifts and falls more restively. I pull the icepacks and go for the kitchen, thinking this small move will be enough to demystify what's happened. Justin will wake from a bad dream, a bruise as soft as a cushion on the back of his head will leave overnight.

Closing the freezer, I spot the wallet again, spread alongside Justin's keys and phone, which hasn't made a noise the entire time. I rifle out the sixty dollars and put everything else back into Justin's bag. I shove the folds into my pocket and head for the entryway, where Patrice waits on the other side of the door, her image bisected over and over in the panes.

Outside, everything is abandoned, barely a movement anywhere: trafficless, childless. The neighbor's lawn a blaring green, manicured into a frontispiece to distract themselves form the daughters who never call. Our car is still parked on the same length of street, unfazed.

I take a look toward Justin, who seems eternally calm now. I hear Tania's voice wedged in my thoughts:

"Your job isn't to convince someone that they've done something wrong," she says. "It's to find the people who already care."

There will always be more who care, I think, and it means forcing an act that says I cannot be erased; I cannot be contained. It wouldn't last ten days, even if they tried.

Patrice and I step off the front steps as an SUV pulls up in the opposite direction, taking a sharp leg into the driveway. It parks alongside Justin's car in one rushed motion, and I feel Patrice's arm fold into the bend of mine and tighten. She tugs for us to move off the lawn, but I anchor us there.

From the car, a woman emerges, doubtlessly a mother, pilates-thin, a necklace with a glinting pendant suspended at the middle of her body. She smiles, undeterred by the idea of us in her yard, and I watch as her purse drops off her shoulder.

"Can I help you?" the woman asks.

The Paragon
of Animals

Aimee and I are realistic people. We're the same kind of grounded. Predictable, some would say. For our third anniversary, we bought an SUV—a Jeep Cherokee, a brand-new Jeep Cherokee with all the bells and whistles—but we spent our entire weekend doing so: no dinner, no declarations, no wildflowers. Instead, we went dealership to dealership, switching up the role of test driver, folding back the seats and lying down in its cab. We saw this as an ultimate feature of the Cherokee; to bury its seats into a flat plane where we could hide out from the rain on camping trips, where we could load up a whole world of things we'd bought, things we'd wanted, things that were ours. Not only were kids never on our mind, but "parent" was never on our mind. We wanted ourselves, and we had it.

Two weeks after that, Aimee went to the doctor to find ways for improving her hypotension—usually a hereditary gold mine, but Aimee noticed her blood pressure dropping enough to make her light-headed—and lo and behold: eight weeks. Coming home from work that day, I found her sitting on the porch steps with a glass of wine and a pack of cigarettes, which she held out as I greeted her.

"You're supposed to start smoking in high school," I said. "That way you're done with it by our age."

Aimee only pushed her offerings closer.

"Are you positive?" I asked—flat as that.

Unlike many in our situation, we realized we had options. Financially, legally, we could discreetly exit this event from our life and move forward. We could be forthright and honest in our decision to do so and likely be brought closer by the experience. That was truthfully how we framed our options, where each one, even the ones we've heard to be the most difficult for others, seemed to somehow benefit us.

"And if we keep her?" Aimee asked later that week.

"Her?" I said.

"I don't know why I said that," she said. "It."

"It's not an 'it' to you?"

"I don't know," she said. "I guess I've been thinking more about the idea. Haven't you?"

Confession: I hadn't. I grew up in a structured family with two pious parents and two younger siblings, all the trimmings and fraying conversations inclusive. For whatever reason, it was an order I never wanted.

"Sure," I said. "The idea."

"What if we're supposed to take on the unexpected, what if this is some sort of sign to drag us outside ourselves?"

Not to say that was that, but after Aimee reached this mindset, once she contained the ability for regret, the regret of losing "her" felt monumental. So yes, that was that.

The summer after Alex's eighth birthday, he was diagnosed with night tremors. A condition that came with a grocery list of symptoms: uncontrollable jerking, sleepwalking, babbling; each morning-after bringing the apportioned consequence: sore muscles, unexplained bruising, a three-hundred-dollar subscription to an Icelandic Rosetta Stone podcast, because Aimee was so convinced the babbles were anything but.

"I forget what it's called," she said, "but it happens. Innate language exposure that swirls in the mind, resurfacing on deathbeds, a midlife crisis, some congenital backlog."

It was three weeks of nightly lessons on her phone before the idea was abandoned.

The most the doctor who diagnosed Alex could offer was a blanket of sleep aids and a recommendation for a local sleep study expert—expert relative for the only local sleep studier.

"What about something more directed?" I asked.

"Directed?" the doctor repeated.

"Prescribed," Aimee chimed in.

"I'm sorry. He's much too young for medical remediation," she said.

On the ride home from the doctor, Alex knocked at the backs of our seats with his wobbly legs, humming aloud a musical number neither of us could place, his headphones cranked up to a lawnmower's decibel.

"Do you know where he gets these songs?" Aim asked.

"No clue," I said. "But it doesn't seem like he'll ever run out."

"Are we supposed to be previewing them, for content or something?"

"I don't think so. I mean he can read. We'd have to start redacting books, right?" to which Aim agreed, though more possibly she was scanning the shelves of her brain for the last book she read with something questionable in it, a pop-up book of human genitalia or some other novelty you accumulate through sheer existence.

"Is medical remediation even a phrase? It sounds foggy," she said.

I knew what she meant, and agreed, but had my ears pointed toward Alex, who had transitioned to a ballad and clapped shut his eyes. He turned moony, almost obscene for this music. It was seven years of tractor-trailers and assembling miniaturizations of the sky-line, and then one class play led to one summerlong theater camp and it all swelled into this mesmerizing love affair. An eight-year-old's undeniable soul mate.

But Jesus Christ if he didn't have the worst singing voice imaginable.

"What do you think of the sleep study?" Aim asked. Honestly, I'd grown accustomed to the simpler routines, the melatonin fruit smoothies, the shots of tart cherry juice, the meandering narration of *Great Expectations*. It was slow, laughable progress but progress nonetheless. Still, when your eight-year-old walks in on his babysitter as she self-satisfies in your living room well past midnight, all directions seem overdue.

"Whatever it takes," I said.

By thirty weeks, Aimee and I had concluded all former routines and introduced a new, magnanimous outlook on life. A child would change us, we knew, but we were going to source it differently. Our child, now certainly a boy, would be our dynamo. His existence, we decided, would be a sneaky fountain of youth. Perhaps there was going to come a day when we wanted a kid, it was certainly reasonable. However, with our previous mindsets, let's say we're 40 when that day creeps in. At that age, we would likely be doomed to spend all our money just to achieve a kid, naturally or otherwise, and once that kid arrives we're low-60s when they're getting through college. That's retirement. Or, if it's not retirement, it's the age at which all you think about is retirement, is escaping demand. Alternately, your child, your life-force, is finally done with the murk of college and is embarking on life. What do you even talk about other than jealousy? What do you drink with them besides table wine? What do you even have the energy to let them teach you?

Fuck all of that, we said. Kicking off unexpectedly would mean we're on quarterlife crisis number two when our son hits the fun ages. We'll be ripe for their journey. Our comedowns will be right as they merge into those contemplations of savings portfolios and joy management. What's more, by the time they're ready to have their own human mistakes, we'll be at that sweet spot of early-onset retirement when we've seen all of Europe, or at least some national parks, and all we want is to act sweetly in a single-level home under the balm of the sun.

Or that was what we told each other. That was what we said in moments of uncertainty. That was how we coped, by giving it a positive charge we were both too chicken-shit to actually touch for fear it would disintegrate us.

In one week, Alex received three detentions for sleeping in class, prompting a call home from his teacher, Ms. Lamb.

"Sometimes kids this age are night owls. Maybe he's playing video games, or overstimulating himself," she suggested.

Aimee had taken the call and relayed the conversation to me after in cryptic, probing notes.

"Do you play video games?" she asked.

"Eleven years together and you don't know if I play video games?"

"What about Alex, does he play them?"

"We don't even own video games," I said.

"I mean online."

"I don't know," I said. "Maybe," because honestly, maybe he did. Alex once closed shut my laptop and told me I needed to update Javascript.

"Do you ever look at the history on his iPad?" she asked. To which I realized no, because neither of us do, because the idea of scrolling through links about off-Broadway shows doesn't much appeal to me. Though, like many traps in parenting, not doing so suddenly felt irresponsible, and so that night I did look. I waited till after he'd gone to bed, and flipped open his iPad. Obviously, there was nothing to consider. According to his usage, he spent all day on the YouTube app and playing chess. All my sleuthing yielded was the fact that my son knows how to play chess.

"Then what's up?" Aim wanted to know. "Why is he sleeping in class?"

Naturally, that answer developed quickly, but understanding his sleeplessness was more of a ghost story.

Each night, we began to open the door to his room every couple hours to monitor his movements, which were jumpy and uncoordinated, not the universal sensation of falling or a few nighttime kicks. The poor kid was running from bats. For a week or so, we took turns waking him up, rubbing circles across his back, calming him asleep: parents of the year.

The next week, Aim was getting home late from a dinner, near midnight, and we were drowsily leaning on the kitchen island with one shared spoon shoved into a pint of ice cream when Alex emerged from the stairs.

"Hey hon, can't sleep?" Aim said to him, but of course he didn't reply. He went over to the pantry, knocked down a few boxes of cereal like a raccoon and went back for his room, only to trip on the second step and wake himself to shock and tears. Next, I installed a baby gate, putting it out at night once Alex was behind closed doors so as to not shame him. An added routine, but an easy fix, and for a few weeks we either rubbed circles or redirected him back to bed when he wandered into ours, like human bumper cars.

And then came the babbles, the screams, the spasms, the ungraceful somnabulance—until it all devolved into a nightly argument of will it or won't it pass, which, I'll admit, I thought it would pass. I truly thought it would pass.

At week thirty-eight, Aimee and I were standing in the bathroom, her favorite nightgown tossed over her shoulders accentuating every day of every week she'd been pregnant, when her water broke. Obviously, I couldn't gauge this event, and Aimee, ever the biology teacher, wasn't about to be overwhelmed, but still; she finished brushing her teeth, peeled off her nightgown, pulled on the elastic pants she had elected for such an event, and said:

"I'm early. Let's go."

She was already at the car when the frenzy hit me, and I was halfway running red lights, trying my best to recall what breaking early entails, the risks involved. Though, honestly, just about every fucking thing seemed like a potential hazard. Improper inductions, arrhythmia, abnormal effacing—all the phrases I learned in preparation for this day came with subsets of complications, family trees of disaster. Even the hospital was repeatedly cautioned as a singles bar for nosocomial infections, which I learned to pronounce seamlessly.

By the time the doctors had filed in to address the situation, I was pulling facts from the air: best route to induce early, antibiotics to prevent infection, possibly steroids, epidural window smaller and smaller, get it going, the baby's coming. The baby's coming, we both heard clearly and pinched our hands together until they were clay.

From there, it was a smooth descent. Not to metaphor, but the doctor was exactly the kind of pilot you want—she had supportive language, a steady form, this bizarre occupational arrogance that said no one else on the face of the planet can do this; this was her job, and it would be her life or our son's.

I kept one hand with Aimee and both eyes peeked around the tent of her legs, followed the commands, watched Alex gift out the center of his mother, and shakily, tearily pushed cheap fabric scissors through a tunnel of membrane like a ribboned announcement, a grand unveiling.

Immediately after, I turned to Aimee. Something about the act of the cut had given me a wonderful twist of pride, and I wanted it seen, but her eyes were shut. Not restfully, but cut off from day, her head stilled in place, and I realized her hand had long stopped holding back. Her blood pressure bottomed out, and the computer screens that had served us so well turned hyper.

The doctor did her best to explain what was happening, but again, I swatted the air: epidurals with low-blood pressure always a risk, mid-delivery would have been a death sentence, don't worry about Alex, Alex will be available soon, Aimee is where she needs to be.

"Do you hear me?" she said, her hands lifting my face off my neck.

"Aimee is where she needs to be," she repeated.

The night that tipped the scales in favor for the sleep study was another anniversary. For the better part of two months, we'd been planning a getaway off-and-on, before ultimately waiting too long and choosing instead a staycation. What was once an illogical move, we dug in deep for: a late dinner, a concert with actual dancing, culminating in an expensive hotel suite. Or, half-suite: the nicest room we could afford.

Our teenage delirium caught up to us in the morning. It had to, honestly. You can't clear 35 and pretend half a dozen shots and a buttery cheeseburger after two market-price fish isn't going to come with repercussions.

Aim rolled over naked except for my underwear—for whatever reason, we'd swapped—and held her phone first far away from her eyes and then so close her nose fogged the screen.

"Mel called," she said.

"Did she text?" I asked, knowing that as long as Mel's been Alex's babysitter, phone calls were rare and texting almost exclusive.

"Just called."

I took my phone from the dresser and saw it was quarter past eleven, a weird limbic hour where we didn't know whether to feel shame or pride. Like children calling their parents after a deceitful night, Aim called back.

The gist of the call was Mel telling Aimee we could talk later.

And while we agreed in the moment, not planning on getting back home until early evening, when Alex was settled down, slipped into movie-watching pajamas, we headed straight home.

On our arrival, Alex greeted us at the garage door, gave us both quick hugs, and darted for the backyard where two neighborhood friends, Marcus and Danny, hung about waiting for the drinks Alex was toting. Not a word about our being home early, or the sight of a potential fever, which Aimee had deduced as a logical case for the phone call.

Mel was sitting on the kitchen island cutting apple wedges and plating them beside turkey sandwiches, her eyes emboldened by our presence.

"Shit," she said, rebounding her words with her hand.

"Shit's fine, Mel," Aimee said, and dropped our overnight bag.

"I didn't mean for you to come home early," she said.

"That's alright," I told her, leaning my weight onto the counter and pulling a sandwich off the plate, eating it from bottom up.

"You sounded off on the phone," Aim said. "What's up?"

Mel transitioned her body off the counter. She's been Alex's main babysitter for three years, and was once Aimee's standout tenth-grade biology student. Her class rank, which cemented her gig as several teachers' regular sitter, was now sending her off to Duke. We had sought to milk the remainder of her summer, but her appearance told us our plans were in jeopardy.

Aimee kicked into teacher mode, and moved closer, and I took my body off my elbows.

"Melanie, what's wrong?" she asked, and Melanie breathed in.

"Last night, it's possible—again, possible—that Alex walked in on me masturbating," she said, one fluid exhale.

Aimee looked toward me with her eyes wide. Not upset, not shock, but displaced. Then, regrouping:

"I'm so sorry," Mel said. "I shouldn't have been—doing that. Here, I mean."

"No, no," Aim tried to reassure, raising a hand in the air as if to wipe the slate clean.

"Right?" she said, motioning in my direction.

"Right," I punctuated. "It was late. And he was asleep, so—"

"Exactly, he was supposed to be asleep and he wasn't. Let's switch to that," Aimee said. "When he walked in, where were you?"

"The couch," Melanie said, to which Aim and I seemed to think in tandem how that was better than a bed, before realizing that it was perhaps not better than a bed at all.

"This couch here?" Aim said, pointing to the living room, but Mel shook her head.

"The front room," she said, referring to the room off the front door, which was admittedly much more tucked an option, and somewhere we'd realized our own urges.

"That sounds like he must have come down the stairs and turned right in," Aim said.

"That sounds like Alex," I said. "Were his eyes open?"

"Dazed, but yes. I said his name. I covered myself up, that is, and said his name. But he didn't respond, just stayed in the room a minute and went back upstairs."

"He walked back upstairs," Aim said defeated. We had very carefully played through the scenarios of Alex's behavior with Mel, explaining it then as a phase, made plans for emergent situations, called the whole thing off each night, and resurfaced in the morning confident it would all be fine; it would be just one night, and it was Mel. The girl was smarter than us.

"Is that bad?" Mel asked.

"He generally isn't coordinated enough to get back up," to which Mel's face flushed.

"Dear—Mel," Aim restructured so as to not coddle. "Were your pants off?"

"They were," Mel said.

"Alright," Aim said. "That's fine, just needed to understand the full picture, but this is fine. It obviously makes sense why you called. I'm sure it feels embarrassing to say aloud."

"I'm so sorry," Mel repeated.

"Don't," Aim said. "It's human," and I nodded. All humans are humans, I thought.

Alex did become available soon, and the nurse assured me I wouldn't miss any update about Aimee by going to see him. He said seeing him might help, explaining how solid his initial vitals were, what that portends; he overstepped, and used the phrase "no matter what." I followed him to the neonatal unit, to a view station for other parents, where he kept his hand at my shoulder as he indicated where Alex lay.

I stared at Alex: his size nothing, his face not sophisticated enough to have expression, small accordion tubes spidering up and down his science fiction container, all routing to a series of readouts that felt too foreign to be good news. I watched as his swaddled shoulders lolled and twitched.

No matter what, Alex would be my future. No matter what, Aimee was his mother. No matter what, I would tell him everything about her and he'd work his entire life to know her. Aimee would become a watercolor on our fridge, a mental fixation when

Alex began to hate me, a lifelong terminal illness. No mater what, I would try to love Alex the way I loved Aimee, but I wouldn't be able. In my own private depths, I didn't even want to try.

Of course, Aimee did recover. The same nurse came and retrieved me from the waiting room, and brought me to her side, where she lay sleeping, stable. He smiled at our reunion, and closed the door. He didn't issue any warnings or directions about how to treat her, nor say not to startle her, or move her, or whether or not she was ever even close to dying. At one point, the doctor entered, saw I was already in the room, and moved on. And I just stayed there until she finally opened her eyes looking for Alex. That was that.

By whatever grand design, the sleep study expert, Victoria, had two open slots: Thursday night, the day before Alex's summer camp performance, or two weeks out, which happened to be Alex's first day back at school. Knowing Aimee, I agreed to Thursday and began copying down the rules of the game. Comfortable pajamas, a favorite pillow, a parent to stay overnight.

After Mel left the house, we began scanning articles about uncovering traumas in children, despite learning that it might be several years if and when Alex's alleged "date night viewing" surfaced as a traumatic event. In other words, we looked where we could, but drowned in qualifiers. One article directed us to ask him what he saw. It suggested we navigate our way through his night, but not ask any questions that might point toward the event. Such interrogation is, unsurprisingly, termed leading the witness, and is apparently as equally a parent's pitfall as it is the police's.

While we sopped up the hangovers brewing inside us, Alex was running to and from the windows of the backyard in pursuit of

Marcus and Danny. In doing so, he attempted his musical theater improv, a skillset he'd previously only workshopped for us.

In short, this practice called for taking a popular number and inserting it into the unexpected—a device made possible by this year's summer camp teacher, Judy. The week before, he was tasked with the assignment of "Danny Boy," and, all week, he'd been belting out this drunkard's tune, sneaking up behind us in the kitchen, popping out of hampers, and breaking into it from start to finish.

Marcus and Danny were tolerant victims until the sun started down, and Alex made his way inside. Collapsed of energy, he slouched at the kitchen table, where we heaped an excessive helping of mac and cheese into his bowl, and sat alongside him, sipping down liters of water.

"You miss us?" Aim asked, to which Alex agreed.

"What'd you and Mel do?" I asked. "Did you sing to her?" and beneath the table, Aimee found my shin, reminding don't lead.

"A little," he said. "I'm sorta shy around her."

"Yeah?" Aim asked. "You didn't seem shy around the boys."

"Those guys don't care about musicals. Melanie watches all of them."

"Melanie's a good listener," Aim said.

"Yeah," Alex agreed, and Aimee tapped me in.

"This is sort of the first time we've left you with someone else all night," I said. "Was it spooky without us?"

"Nope," Alex said, head left and right in decisive twists.

"You feel safe with Melanie, then?" I said, which Aimee didn't seem to love but let pass.

"I guess so," he said, and a gurgle of burp left his chest.

"Maybe she can come to my performance next week," Alex said.

"Would you like her to?" Aim asked.

"Sure," he said. "Judy says a songbird can't be shy when it's his turn to sing."

"We'll invite her," Aimee said, though I understood better that, deep down, she was figuring out a way to eject Judy from our lives for good, and I wanted nothing more than to push the poison in her direction.

"Did you two do anything else?" I asked, feeling our intentions slipping away.

"Uh, we watched *Grease* and a little of the second *Grease*," he said, and Aim and I both nodded eagerly, yearning for him to say more, any vestige of a clue: I didn't sleep well, Melanie doesn't do reading voices as well as you two (a former complaint), why would her pants be off? But no. Just a mustache of powdery cheese hiking up and down.

"Fun!" Aim said at last, and laid her head against the table.

The sleep clinic turned out to be a dentist's office no longer in use, the waiting room converted to an intake room with a small set of lockers. The several available rooms now contained hospital beds where operating chairs were once bolted down, and each room came with an observation porthole cased along the same wall as the door.

I offered to take Alex on my own, to which Aimee eagerly agreed, excited by the prospect of a night without us. She shoved Alex into a pair of pajamas and locked the door.

Victoria toured us down the hallway, letting Alex look in on the other rooms where several patients already dozed, making the process look peaceful and safe.

"Alex," she said. "Did your dad explain what we do here?"

"Yes. You watch my dreams and look out for anything suspicious," he said, which Victoria seemed to both like and dislike with one smile.

"Here's you," she said, patting the bed. As Alex reclined back, she gave him a remote to adjust the mattress to his liking.

"Play as much as you want. You'll want to be comfortable."

Alex immediately folded himself into a V-shape before flattening back out, telling us he liked the way we have his bed at home.

"The next step," Victoria explained, "is putting on sensors."

Demonstrating on me, she began to affix the patches to my temples, my heart, my neck.

"They take your pulse from all directions," she said.

"Like stethoscopes," Alex said.

"Exactly," she said. "Okay, I need to check a few dream results. I'll be back in a minute."

Alex dismissed her and I peeled off the stickers. He laid his head back and yawned big, just as he often did at home attempting to stay awake as long as us, his fight always ending with his head collapsed in one of our laps. For years, we'd allowed this. Despite the parenting books, the parents-in-law, the cohorts of parenting friends, all insisting upon us the same concept, that a child's biology loves structure.

"Alex," I said, and he rolled his face across the pillow to see me.

"What."

"Are you nervous?"

"A little," he said.

"Would it help if we talked through it?"

"Can we sing?"

"Sing?"

"Yeah. I like to sing more than talk."

"You get that from your mom."

"You don't like to sing?" he asked, which imparted both pain and joy, as I thought back on the past year's mimed rendition of Happy Birthday.

"I've just never had a good voice."

"Judy says it's not about the voice, it's about the courage behind it," to which I nodded.

"Melanie told us she loves hearing you sing. Are you going to miss her when she leaves for school?"

"Yeah," he said, and rolled his head back to the ceiling. "I love her."

"You do?" I asked, to which Alex shook his head, not understanding my response to be a question of more.

"How long have you felt that way?" I repeated.

Alex shrugged. "Always."

He inflected the word as if "to love" is the default, that a person may fall out of love, but the falling-in is implied—all it takes is acknowledging the person in front of you.

"Okay dad," Victoria said, reentering. "Let's have you go out so Alex can get some sleep," and she quickly began attaching new pads to the sensors, swabbing each with a gummy liquid.

I leaned over top Alex and kissed his head.

"Sleep tight, bud," and his arms lifted up pretending to be a robot, collapsing around my neck with a tight, mechanical squeeze.

Through the window, I watched as Victoria finished patching Alex up and down, pointing to the machines around the room, the camera in the corner through which she'd be watching, the help button should he need to reach her, and she brushed her fingers through his hair in one meditative sweep before dimming the lights.

In the hall, Victoria closed the door with familiar skill, and stepped toward me. "You don't have to wait here," she said. "We have a room for you, too. No cameras, I promise."

"Is it alright if I stay a while longer?" I asked.

Victoria brought me a chair to sit in, but its legs weren't tall enough to allow me to see in, so that I continued to stand outside the room, peering in like a ghost.

Behind the glass, Alex was rumpled down in lowlight, a small network of wires hanging off his frame and mapping his life. I imagined Victoria a few rooms over positioned in front of her monitors, long ribbons of printouts piling up across her feet with Alex's brainwaves, Alex's heartbeats, Alex's lyrics.

It transported me to years before in the neonatal unit. How after Aimee had awoken in the emergency room, her heart stable, the world whole, she had fallen back asleep. I stared at her for nearly an hour, questioning the rise and fall of her chest, before leaving the room to find Alex again. This painful memory still caught in my arms from when I thought Aimee was gone forever, from a time in which she was being exchanged for him. I remember standing in the unit, his body through the window only a nose poking out of fabric.

I stood wondering how long it would be before I agreed to love him.

Tennessee

I can't point to the moment in time my mother officially relinquished logic, but I can compare the instances: I can catalog crazy, as it were. Make no mistake, the candidacy of these occurrences, over a very short period, had become substantial. My mother robbed hardware stores, sexually assaulted a young man bagging her groceries, ate my father, and placed me in credit card debt. And, yes, that's the order I retell it—not based on the dramas that ensued, but in a chronology I am at least privy to owning.

Yet, in the backyard, the spade tip of the shovel half-eaten in the dirt, and I can probably name what disappeared her for good.

My father was not my old man, but my very old man. My mother was over twenty years his junior, and by the time she had me, her only biological possession, she was already too old to be doing so. Of the situation, my uncle would often restate to me, once he felt I was of an age old enough (twelve):

"Fuck all, if I didn't think you were going to come out of her gangly and slow."

Though, this is arguably a poor manner by which to introduce my Uncle Andy. Andy, my mother's younger brother, who took me to sports games as a kid, who drove me to my college orientation, who built the small rowboat by hand on which I proposed to Ellie. Fuck all, if he wasn't the person who raised me.

Of course, Andy's position in my life was always attributed to my father's predetermined age and frailty. While other children's fathers were apparent, attendant, mine was in the lobby in a wheelchair, plastic pinched into his nose so that oxygen could canal up. He died a week before I hit eighteen, and on his deathbed, he said nothing to me, or anyone else.

In many ways, this was where the bolt loosened.

I went away to college, and my mother was left alone, so that any minimal transition I could have seen coming, any vestige of something being wrong, her coordination mismatched, of salt in the sugar, was overlooked in my not being around.

On the day I loaded the last duffel into Andy's truck and headed for school, my mother: in her nightgown, in the early morning outside the green brick house that raised me, told me,

"Girls are trouble, but grandchildren are a mother's dream."

She pulled me in tight, her chin somehow resting on top of my head, despite my being taller, the dun skin of her elbows denting out the papery, floral print. I kissed her on the cheek, and was likely kissing her goodbye.

◉

Ellie is the most patient person I've ever met. She could watch our car being stolen, and she would take my hand and patently say,

"No need to panic."

In our second year of college, Ellie's father—who I had met more than once, but never as Ellie's boyfriend, only as the shy, sycophantic friend who helped unload his Ford Explorer—suffered a stroke, which left one side of his body useless.

I drove Ellie to the hospital to see him, took her tears to my shoulder when the prognosis returned, the fabric later crinkled from everything that came out of her. Yet, it was in this moment where I learned where Ellie became Ellie.

The hospital, with its quietly eroding wallpaper, with its news channels stuck on the TV, with the parade of squeaky shoes, and Ellie's father: before he was wheeled out, he had tied a string around his unusable wrist, and with his good hand, was pulling the string into the air to salute doctors and nurses goodbye, ventriloquist and man fused. If Ellie's father were anything, he was, complementally, the youngest.

My mother's first episode appeared in the form of a dead mouse from the garage, who she'd bought a cage for, had put a tiny doll's hat on, and whose water and food she appeared to be replacing. A sharp smell overtook the noses of both Ellie and me, the afternoon I introduced her to my mother. Yet, it was Ellie, in the politest voice, who asked of the cage,

"Does this little guy have a name?"

I threw the mouse out, sprayed the cage with scented aerosol, put it back in the garage, scrubbed everywhere I felt the mouse could have emitted whatever the hell a dead mouse emits, and Ellie held my mother, who sat mourning my actions.

It was the fall semester of my senior year, and, before this, I thought my mother's crazy amounted to overlong conversations, to marrying a man too old to stay awake at the movies.

In subsequent months, I began to receive phone calls. Each more unpredictable than the last, to a point that my imagination evolved enough to shrink the problems with every answer.

It's always the case in horror movies that the manner in which a person is punished or gruesomely killed off is elaborate. No longer is it enough to see the shower curtain shadow. We need a depth to the hideousness. If someone's fingernails are pulled off in a torturous manner, we know it's bad, we do; but we know it's worse if boiling water is poured over what's exposed.

In many ways, then, the phone calls became just that. The person on the other end, often a police officer, or a store manager:

"We found your mother's trunk filled with hammers. Our security tapes have her stealing two to three a day for almost a month."

I wouldn't protest, I wouldn't apologize, I would wait on the line for what my mother intended to do with the hammers, for the modifier that took the situation out of the shallow end of tragic and into that deep end, where skin blistered.

"Hello?"

"I'm sorry," I said. "Would you put her on?"

"Hi, sweetie."

"Hi, mom. So, what's with all the hammers?"

"I don't know, I just kept forgetting we had one, I guess."

"How many hammers do you have?"

"In the car and at the house?"

And this was the point of departure, my routine four-hour drive home and four-hour drive back to my apartment, an imprint of sweat lining the cell phone in my pocket. It became the most burdensome thing I owned that tiny device, and it glowed warmly all day, like a gun or stack of money: something no one else could know you have, but the possession of which feels acidic.

The night we went to my mother's and announced that Ellie was pregnant, we wrapped a helium balloon into a large box, and tied a sinker and the sonogram to the end of the string. When she opened it, the balloon would rise and hold perfectly in place at her eyeline. I knew, because I tweaked the process for hours, tying different knots, different lengths of string, different counterbalances. I opened the box at least twenty times watching the image of our baby come at me. For a time, I even thought this was birth, the lid as Ellie's legs, the hollow Ellie's stomach, our child rising impossibly out, cut the string and the memory of something once inflated disappears skyward.

Ellie wrapped her arms around me in the kitchen.

"Are you ready, we'll be late if you fiddle any more."

"How big is the little one now?" I asked, my hand resting above Ellie's navel.

"A lime."

"Fiesta baby. When's the banana?"

"Not for a while."

"It's a very odd shape to compare a child to."

"Don't even remind me, I'd rather it was ready to go when it was the size of a raspberry."

We had moved into a small duplex not two miles away from my mother the year after graduation. On warm nights, Ellie and I preferred to walk our streets, the blur of magnolia trees kept beneath dying lights to map us. The features of night so stilling, they were like pieces of felt ironed up alongside our way. When the moon was whole, it felt like day, and when it went unseen, the stars numbered so many they looked like pinches of salt that could brighten molasses. In this repetition, there was always calm, always an understanding between the part of the universe you can't touch and us.

Ellie, since the day her pregnancy was confirmed, had begun relentlessly reading children's books, wanting to create the most developed library she could manage. I blamed it on her majoring in semiotics; she saw it as necessary for our child to be smarter than us, as if there are parents actually more intelligent than their children.

A story she once read aloud imagined a world without gravity, so that people eventually stopped aging, no longer bore down by the physics of time, they floated upward: they lived forever in the sky children and together.

It was a short book, but it moved Ellie to tears. Initially, I thought it had to do with her father, who had passed only months before, this time to a heart attack.

"It's appalling," she said aloud.

"What is?"

"That the world should end here, with people not old enough to do anything, forced to tie themselves down, to live in fear of floating away."

What frightened her didn't exactly strike me. I took it as a children's story: simple premise, cute idea, the flowing calligraphy of pastel faces to amuse big eyes. I hadn't seen it as premonitory, as a story of an ethereal soup where everything stood in place, but it made me think that Ellie felt the world in a way I never had, but that sometimes my mother did.

When we arrived, box in hand, the kitchen table was set as usual, with one additional placemat overseeing the others. At the head of the table, near the backdoors of the kitchen, was my father's urn, its object silvery and contained, positioned before a plate of biscuits and flash-grilled pork chop.

"Mom, is dad joining us tonight?"

"Well, why not? Rather rude of us to not invite him over from the mantle."

Ellie and I took our seats and said grace waywardly, but were too anxious to begin eating. My mother split a biscuit in half and looked over toward our peering faces, as the steam separated the dough.

"Not hungry? Oh, was it not cooked enough, is it undercooked?" and she carved into the meat, terrified by the prospect.

"Mom, Ellie and I found you a present, we were wanting you to open it."

"Oh yeah? Where is it?"

From the hall, I grabbed the box, its bow perfectly tied at the center, its cardboard panels sheen and rose. I moved over her plate and put it before her like the main course. My mother smiled big, popped the rest of her biscuit in her mouth, and wiped the little grease and flour chalk on the sides of her pants.

She grinned again, and lifted the lid. The balloon sailed straight up and into the ceiling fan behind her, and exploded in one sensational pop. It startled Ellie, who moved away from the noise, knocking my father's urn into the air, and we all listened as it rolled against the tile of the kitchen floor.

The urn was empty, dry to the touch. I picked it up in disbelief, thinking as soon as Ellie's hand touched the pewter that I would have to spend the night putting my father into the same dustbin we used to collect mites and hair, attaching the vacuum's extensions to suck him up off the rug, and immediately sifting through the bag for the human ends.

"Mom, where the hell are the ashes?"

"I ran out of flour."

We looked to our plates.

"Mom. You didn't."

And as the words broke from me, the idea splitting open the already flimsy architecture of lungs and heart, my mother picked up the sonogram from the floor.

"A lime! It's already a lime!"

Ellie, still painfully caught off-guard, removed herself to the upstairs bathroom, and my mother's arms slinked over my shoulders. I could nearly feel my phone vibrating in my pocket, the pull of logic calling to tell me the movie was over.

As usual, Andy was the first person we told, but his advice was always the same. Five minutes into the living room, the sonogram on the table in front of him, he said,

"She can't live alone. If you weren't having a baby, I'd say she could live with you. Now, I work in too many different places. I have a few more years before I can collect a dime, and I don't think we have a few more years."

"I can't just commit her."

"This isn't the old world, it's not some barren asylum. They have nice places, they do. There's one up past Arawata, called Fenwick Gardens. Pretty affordable, a guy I work with had his wife set up there when her dementia came on too strong."

I looked over to Ellie, who, in my mind, was already cradling her stomach at eight months, and shouldn't be moving too suddenly—but she was still. No fish bowl of skin, no convex pulse, no talked-about glow. Her face was drawn downward, and I knew that this was Ellie's patience running out.

Fenwick Gardens had what they deemed an on-call system: a landline, which would dial immediately out to every pager in the place as soon as the phone was picked up. Esme, a woman with a thick, caramel accent, was the nurse most often in charge of my mother's floor. She had tumid, softball hands, and wore small, gold earrings, which rippled like an accordion, for every shift.

On move-in day, Esme shouldered the two of us through the routine, seeming to pause at the times when she anticipated questions she'd been asked before, asked a dozen times by the others who were in this room, this bed, this impersonation.

The room available for my mother was shelved in attributes: flowers that appeared daily replaced, green virginal bulbs enveloped around a nib of color; mint-toned walls; wax shades over the windows, disfiguring the sky; a table with four chairs where she could play tea with her nightly mise-en-scène; a doorless bathroom.

The next room over, an aggravated knocking thwacked away, like a head falling asleep and dropping onto a desk, over and over. Esme smiled at us both, a parent overwhelmed with embarrassment.

I looked to my mother, who was not angry, or rundown, excited, or reactive in any way. She was simply herself confronting truth.

When I was eleven, before all his driving privileges were suspended, my father took me to see a minor league game in Knoxville. My mother, whole-hearted, full-minded, loaded the car with everything short of emergency flares and the act of tattooing our phone number to my arm. I expected she felt that if anything happened to either of us, it would be her fault, her setup.

On the road, the several hours we had to drive there and back, my father was mostly quiet, the croon of radio and the ripple of wind from the windows rolled down the only dissipations of noise. And then he came to me with an openness I only experienced on that drive.

"You remember Julia?" he said.

For seven years, my father played minor league baseball, at third, a position which you need a pitcher's arm and a leadoff's speed to compete at, as he intoned over and over to me in the decade we knew each other. He moved from Charleston to Baton Rouge to El Paso to Kansas City to Cincinnati to Memphis. He met his first wife on the road, and his second the same way. The second wife, Janine, was also much younger, also supposedly alive. They exchanged Christmas cards, and nothing else. The first wife, however, the one my father never spoke of, and who I believed only my mother knew of as silhouette, was the person I imagined had actually observed my father's youth, his truest self: Julia.

"She was taller than your mother, taller than me, maybe. She played in the girls' league. I came back after the war, and started to play again, too. We started to have a go of things. Her playing died down when men's leagues were back, and I wasn't good enough to be good. Sort of just fizzled out there in the field. Julia left, too. Took up with a salesman. Died a few years later in a car accident."

Until that day, I hadn't known my father was a veteran. The paraphernalia of such eras was crammed into the crawl spaces of our house, and an old flag folded to a triangle was displayed in our upstairs hall, but it was the flag laid over the casket of my father's brother: a man shot down flying over Poland. There was no talk of my father going, and his relatives were either too old to remember a full sentence, or so old they remembered the war with such living clarity it seemed impossible I wouldn't know.

That afternoon, we never made it to the ballpark. My father went unobserved through a stop sign, and a gravel truck clipped the rear corner of the car. We didn't skid or flip, but it tipped us on our side, like the slow roll of whale. I slid midair toward his seat, my seatbelt catching me like the harness of a bungee. The driver's side window shattered on the pavement, a small collision from somewhere giving my father a nosebleed. He pulled out his handkerchief to hold the clot, and looked over to me as I squirmed against gravity to climb out of the door.

"Son," he said. "No need to panic."

When Ellie's stomach was a grapefruit, we took the sonogram to my mother. She was distant, but calm; she was the portrait of the mother I remember clearest, eyes wide and agate in the sun. Though, I understood this was her in medicated daze.

She held Ellie's hand and touched her stomach.

"It's kicking!" she said, but Ellie and I had yet to feel a kick. Ellie put her hand against the stomach, and I did the same, the small, ovoid pouch like a reservoir: it somehow felt more still to me than ever before.

"She is, kicking just for you," Ellie told her. My mother loved these words, they left her overrun with joy and possibility and images of the throat of her hand beneath the baby's armpits.

The day before, we had had Andy over for dinner. He had just been to Fenwick, and he held my shoulder in the kitchen of my childhood home. Since moving my mother out, Ellie and I had sublet our apartment at a slight profit to try and help cover the difference insurance wouldn't. We put new carpeting in the bedroom of my mother's room, repainted the walls of the kitchen, even the molding; we did our best to eradicate all of my connection to it. Yet, something still didn't feel right.

"You see her recently?" he asked.

"Just yesterday."

"She's rambling again."

"Anything specific?"

"No, just rambling. She was trying to tell me she needed tools, that she needed things fixed up."

"What fixed up?"

"I don't know. So I went out to the truck, I grabbed my box, and I went back in. I asked her, 'What's the problem?' but she said, 'Not here, the other house. The other house.'"

"You think something over here is broken?" I asked him.

"Don't know, but I think you and I might take a look after dinner. She's not all crazy."

We did just that, moving to and from the corners of the basement steps, pilot lights to air ducts, our hands in and out of everywhere. In the attic, I found the memorabilia of my father's time in war, of his time playing baseball; I found what was probably a picture of Julia, dust in its creases. But, the house, for its age, was fine.

In the paint-by-numbers living room of my mother's apartment, she sat with one ankle behind the other, not speaking unless spoken to, seeming nearly resentful, like a child who takes their punishment with a smile. I leaned beside the phone, imagining the anxiety Esme must feel with all lines now routed to her.

Another hour passed, and Ellie started to feel unwell. We wrapped up the muffins we'd brought for my mother to have in the morning. We kissed her on the cheek, and when my head was just close enough to her lips, she whispered,

"Don't forget to fix up the backyard, now."

I paused, and waited for Ellie to reach the door. I knelt my head toward my mother.

"What's in the backyard?"

"Our mementos," she said, still softly, as if these were mine and hers, not something for Ellie or our daughter to cherish. And then time hit me.

My mother was nearly ritualistic when it came to tradition. There was order and not compromise, and she enjoyed greatly any opportunity for a regular day to be one we marked on the calendar. She was also prone to superstition.

I wasn't yet ten, I believe, and my mother woke me from my bed one night, the sound of my father's snoring, of his oxygen machine cooing in the next room over the first thing I heard before her voice.

"Come with me," she said, and I followed her down to the back-doors of the kitchen, where she had our shoes waiting.

Outside, a shovel leaned against the wooden steps, and the moon large and freckled sat suspended above us, like the bottom of a straw hole that would soon suck up the night and make day. From the pocket of her robe she removed a ring box and held it out to me.

"Once a year, on a full moon, it's good luck to bury the past," she said, "You're old enough now to continue the tradition with me."

With the spear of shovel, I broke into the earth, dug past soil, past loam, and into gravel. She dropped in the box, and I poured it all back over in the very same order of strata. When it was done, my mother took my head to her lips, and leaned me beneath her armpit. I could remember her reaching up to the sky, her hand covering the moon in my vantage, and she squeezed her wrist like closing off a symphony.

The next morning, it was simply our secret, though she never had me dig again.

I kissed my mother, her face pallid and small.

"I won't forget," I told her, and I followed Ellie toward the car.

In the backyard, beneath the wooden steps, beat down from the weather and murk that landed on top of them, I find three shovels, all different sizes and lengths, all caked with dirt and heft.

It's not a full moon, but it's close to: it's a fraction away. Ellie is in bed now, reading, and I haven't shared with her the memory trapped between my eyes. Though, I know that when I inevitably do, she'll pick up a shovel and stand beside me. For the moment, I want it as my own, as something that may be the last sane tunnel between me now and who my mother was. I think it again: me now she was.

I pace the yard, trying to circle the area my mother and I stood, and I take my first guess. The dirt upheaves easily, and my no longer being a child, but whatever is a man, speeds the process. I hit gravel in the third shot. I find nothing.

Around me is a half-acre of slick grass, and one hole no wider than a bucket. Somewhere, sunk inside me, though rising up, I know it's not only a ring box. I know that it may be decades more. It may take the whole night, the next day, or longer, but I can feel the possession of my mother beneath me. I know that I'm standing on a place of world that has stopped aging, which has pushed itself into gravity, and has found the same conclusion as a world of children floating to an other place they can't anticipate.

Acknowledgments

In the event this one's it.

Bookside.

To Meg, Kate, Julie, Katherine: it looks like these names are in an order—they are not.

To Katie Freeman: your dedication to prioritizing humanity equally with art is invigorating.

To editors at *American Short Fiction, Glimmer Train, Southern Humanities Review,* and *StoryQuarterly.*

Lifeside.

To Ani Prekker Levine; in both life and writing, I feel precisely nowhere without you.

To Ellen and Mark, and the kitchen table we share; to Rich and Amanda, for filling up its chairs.

To Gal and Stu, who regather me year after year and never ask for anything in return.

To Bryan, whose friendship is indivisible from all the laughter in my life.

To Rachael, for understanding the winning formula behind every great romantic comedy, but more so ensuring there's always a lightness on the East Coast.

To a group of Memphians who opened their doors and windows and fed and drank me under the table like a lost family member.

To Cally Fiedorek, who reads everything first (and I hope vice versa till we're older and grayer).

To Rome and Stephanie, who've been looking after me since 2010 but likely centuries before.

To Reema, an actual confidante through and through.

To Michaela, thank you for always moving the levers of my brain and making me feel sane.

To Kelly. You're not real. You're an absolute ghost.

Lastly, because it's always the real first and foremost: my family, who live on outside all books, and claim me no matter the distance or differences between us.

Adobe Garamond Pro
10.8 / 15.3